Royal Blood Never Fades

The Foundation

Daquian H. Williams

GrindTime Publishing Group, INC
COLUMBUS, OHIO.

This book is intentionally formatted with blank pages to preserve the chapter formatting in print.

Grind Time Publishing Group, Inc.
138 E 5th Avenue
Columbus, Ohio 43201

Ordering Information:
Quantity sales. Discounts are available on quantity purchases by corporations, associations, and others. For details, contact the "Special Sales Department" at the address above.

Royal Blood Never Fades/ Daquian H. Williams. -- 1st ed.
ISBN: 9781967339006
Library of Congress Control Number:2025951019

Dedication

To my bloodline past, present, and future.

The ones who paved the way, the ones who walk beside me, and the ones who will carry this torch when I am gone.
Royal blood runs deep and it never fades.

To Serenity, my heartbeat, my why, my forever. You are the light that guided me through the darkest chapters.
This empire, this legacy it is all for you.

To my father and every soul, I have lost to the streets. Your pain became my purpose. Your silence echoes through every page.

May this story be proof that your memory still moves mountains.

For the Hustlers & Survivors

To the misunderstood, the underestimated, the over-comers. If you have ever been counted out, this one is for you.

You were born royal, even if the world never crowned you.

GrindTime Dedication

To every member of the GrindTime Family.

This foundation was built with struggle, sweat, and relentless dedication and loyalty.

Our code is unbreakable.

Our bloodline, unforgettable.

“Loyalty ain’t in the blood, it is in the decisions. Some of your worst enemies once shared your last name.”

— King GrindTime

Contents

PROLOGUE

The streets don't care who you are.

They don't care about your name, your dreams, or the promises you whisper to yourself late at night.

They'll chew you up and spit you out if you're not built for it.

But me?

I was built for it.

It started with just us.

Just me and wifey who later became Serenity's Mom.

Plus, my brothers from another mother

No riches.

No power.

Just a vision.

I was a young hustler back then, moving pieces across a board nobody even knew existed.

The plan was simple:

Stack up.

Move smart.

Never let emotions cloud judgment.

But the streets?

They never let you play fair.

I remember the first deal that almost got me killed.

Columbus, Ohio.

A warehouse off I-70, late at night. One of those pitch-black hours when you can't see your hand in front of your face.

The kind of night where your momma's voice rings in your head:

> "Ain't nothing good out there at this time."
>
> I learned early that her warning didn't mention one thing! Worms come out at night too.
>
> And those late-night worms are the worms the early bird can't catch

They're the ones that build empires.

The money made it worth the night shifts.

Those quick transactions were steppingstones.

And like all the others, this play was supposed to be clean.

Cash for product.

In and out.

But the second those doors slammed shut behind me...

I knew I'd just walked into a setup.

That night, I learned two things:

1. Never let a man think he has the upper hand.

2. If you want to survive in this game, you better outthink, outmaneuver and when necessary, outgun anyone standing in your way.

This was just the beginning.

Those little dub sacs.

They were the seeds of a dynasty.

A legacy the world would never forget.

Chapter One

Built for This

The penthouse wrapped in silence, not the gentle kind that calms the mind, but the kind that tightens the air before a storm. The city of Columbus sparkled below, but inside this fortress of glass and marble, something was off.

King GrindTime stood before a floor-to-ceiling window, a silhouette of precision and poise. His reflection stared back, dressed in all-black Armani, a rose-gold Rolex gleaming beneath his cuff. But he wasn't admiring the view.

He stood knowing him, his brothers and family owned the view.

Every skyscraper that clawed at the clouds, every nightclub that stayed lit till sunrise, every back-alley deal and uptown transaction if it moved money in Columbus, it moved through them first.

Behind him, the quiet dance of a butterfly knife sliced through the silence. Vincent "Vinnie" Kessler sat perched at the penthouse bar, the blade flipping between his fingers like a magician with a secret to kill.

"Still got it," Vinnie muttered, twirling the knife into its sheath without looking. "But something doesn't feel right tonight."

On the suede couch, Tyrell "Big Ty" Blackhorse leaned back, his hulking frame sprawled out, gold tooth glinting as he scrolled through a burner phone. The glow lit up the sudden tightness in his jaw.

He stopped scrolling.

"We got a problem," Ty said, his voice heavy.

King turned slowly. Not rushed. Just... sharp. His eyes, dark and unreadable, zeroed in as Big Ty tossed the burner onto the marble table.

King stepped forward, picked it up, and scanned the screen.

Encrypted texts.

Photos.

Meet-ups.

Locations.

Someone in the family one of their own was talking to the feds.

Vinnie let out a slow, low whistle. "Somebody done lost their damn mind."

King didn't say a word. He placed the phone down gently, as if it was made of glass. Then adjusted his cuff, smoothing out the silk.

"Who?" His voice was silk over a blade.

Big Ty cracked his knuckles like thunder. "Rico."

A long silence stretched.

The same man who helped bury bodies. Who stood by them in gunfights. Who toasted with King after they took over their first block. Rico was Family.

King nodded once. “You sure?”

“Burners registered to his side chick,” Big Ty said. “I traced it twice. Same contact names we used in our last run. Time stamps match the shipment schedule.”

King’s jaw twitched. “Then it’s not just betrayal. It’s intent.”

Vinnie leaned forward, voice cold. “What’s the move?”

King walked toward the glass again, looking out into the night. Lights blinked across the skyline like signals in Morse code. Somewhere out there, Rico was breathing.

Too long.

He turned. “Bring him in.”

Vinnie grinned. “I was hoping you’d say that.”

He stood, cracked his neck, and slipped out the door without another word.

Big Ty sighed, rubbing his face. “Damn shame. Rico’s girl just had a baby last week.”

King stared at the burner phone like it owed him answers. “Then she’ll understand what betrayal costs.”

Ty nodded, no hesitation. “There’s rules.”

The elevator dinged softly. The doors slid open.

In walked Julius "Jules" GrindTime King's second eldest. No chains. No loud energy. Just tailored sharp, laptop bag slung over his shoulder, and a mind that could break Wall Street with a side-eye.

"Pop," Jules said, tossing a folder onto the table. "Accounts in Zurich and Dubai are clean. But we've got an issue down in Miami."

King raised an eyebrow. "Talk to me."

"The Vasquez Cartel's trying to buy out clubs we marked last quarter. They moved quick. Too quick."

Big Ty sat up straighter. "Vasquez? Ain't they the ones from the port wars?"

Jules nodded. "Same ones. They wanna push us out."

King smiled. Not a friendly smile. The kind of smile that signaled the beginning of something very, very dangerous.

"Good."

Big Ty blinked. "Good? How the hell is that good?"

King's smile widened as he turned back toward the city.

"Because now we got an excuse... to take everything they own."

Ty leaned back, smirking. "This finna be fun." The room stayed quiet but this time, it wasn't storm-brewing silence.

It was the sound of wolves licking their chops.

Chapter Two

No Loose Ends

The warehouse on the east side of Columbus was cold, forgotten, and quiet except for the occasional drip of water from a cracked pipe above. A single bulb swung from a chain, casting warped shadows across the concrete walls like ghosts watching from the dark.

In the center of the room sat Rico Alvarez.

His wrists zip-tied to a steel chair, blood crusted at the corner of his mouth, a deep bruise blooming across his cheekbone. His lips trembled. Sweat beaded down his temple despite the chill. His eyes darted around the warehouse like he could still find a way out.

But there was no way out.

King GrindTime stood a few feet away, dressed in all black. Not a wrinkle on his custom fit. Not a single emotion on his face.

He didn't need to yell.

He didn't need to threaten.

King's silence was the punishment.

Across the room, Vinnie leaned against a rusted support beam, arms crossed. He toyed with a thin wire like he was flossing. Big Ty paced behind Rico, cracking his knuckles, the floor creaking under his weight.

Rico's voice cracked as he broke the silence. "King... King, please. I-I didn't mean to"

King raised a hand slowly, cutting him off without a word.

He walked forward and pulled up a chair, the legs scraping against the cement floor. He sat down directly across from Rico. His voice was quiet. Controlled.

"I'm going to ask you one question," King said. "And you get one chance to answer it right."

Rico swallowed hard. "I swear on my kid's life, I didn't"

King sighed and rubbed his temple. "Wrong answer."

The bulb above flickered, the chain rattling.

King leaned in, voice barely above a whisper. "Why'd you do it?"

Rico's lips trembled. "They had my family. My baby girl, man. They said if I didn't feed them information, they'd hurt them. I didn't know what else to do..."

King nodded slowly. He looked down for a moment, then raised his eyes again calm, cold, final.

"Did you think to come to me first?"

Rico's silence said everything.

King exhaled. "You made a decision. And decisions come with weight."

Big Ty stepped forward, his gold tooth catching the light. "You coulda said somethin', Rico. We protect our own. You know that."

Rico shook his head desperately. "I was scared"

"You should've been," Vinnie said flatly from the shadows.

King stood, smoothing the sleeves of his coat. He took a few steps back, then paused, hands behind his back.

"Loyalty isn't optional," he said softly.

Rico started to cry, chest heaving, snot running down his nose.

"Please, King. I'm beggin' you."

King looked over at Vinnie.

One nod.

The gunshot cracked like thunder.

Rico's body slumped, the chair wobbling, then tipping over with a metallic crash. Blood pooled beneath him thick, dark, silent.

Big Ty wiped his mouth with a cloth napkin, like he just finished dinner. "No loose ends."

King stared at the body for a long moment.

Then turned and walked out, his voice echoing as he spoke to no one in particular

"Bag him. Burn the chair."

" You don't get a second chance with loyalty.

You either come real or stay gone."

Chapter Three

Mama GrindTime

The room smelled like cookies, incents, Mary Jane and Black & Mild smoke. The kind of smells that let you know you were home. King GrindTime sat at the long wooden dining table, his fingers tapping against the glass of Tequila in front of him with a blunt in his hand. Across from him sat Mama GrindTime the foundation, the backbone, the woman who had endured more storms than most could survive.

Her silver-streaked braids pulled back, her eyes sharp as ever. Age hadn't dulled her presence; if anything, it made her even more powerful. The kind of woman whose silence could say more than a thousand words.

She set down her perfectly rolled joint and leaned forward. "I heard about Rico."

King didn't flinch. "Handled."

She nodded slowly, taking a sip of her tea. "I ain't worried about how you handled it, boy. I'm worried about what's next."

King sighed, rolling his shoulders. “Miami is next ma; it's just a slight hiccup with the Vasquez Cartel in the way.”

Mama GrindTime smirked. “Mmhmm. And you think they the only ones watching?”

Big Ty, sitting off to the side, chuckled. “Mama, you already know King.”

She shot him a look. “Ain’t nobody questioning’ shit but his stubborn ass going listen.’ Power ain’t just about what you do, it’s about who’s watching when you do it.”

King let her words settle. She was right. She always was.

She exhaled slowly, eyes drifting back to him. “I built you for this. You built this empire. But don’t get so high up that you forget who’s still waiting’ in the shadows.”

Vinnie walked in at that moment, wiping his hands with a towel. “Brother, the jet's ready. We rolling?”

King stood up, adjusting his suit. “Yeah. Time to collect what’s ours.”

Mama GrindTime stood too, walking over and straightening his collar like he was still her little boy, and not the most powerful man in the streets.

She looked him in the eyes. “You remember what I told you?”

King nodded. “Never swing first.”

She smiled. “That’s right. Make ‘em think they are winning’. Then bury ‘em.”

“ Trust is earned. Loyalty is tested. Betrayal is remembered.”

Chapter Four

Blood in the Soil

The jet wheels hit the tarmac with a soft hiss, but the tension in the cabin was anything but smooth.

King GrindTime sat at the head of the jet's leather lounge section, legs crossed, blunt lit, eyes half-closed as the Miami skyline came into view through the tinted window. He wasn't sightseeing.

He was calculating.

Next to him, Big Ty was already halfway through a Cubano sandwich, chewing like he didn't have a care in the world. But his other hand rested casually on a black duffel bag zipper half-open, revealing enough firepower to flatten a small city block.

Across from them, Vinnie cleaned his pistol with the same calm a man might use to butter toast. He glanced up.

"You smell that, boys?"

Big Ty raised an eyebrow. "Smell what?"

Vinnie grinned, gold tooth flashing.

"Fear. Opportunity. Coconut oil. Whatever the hell Miami reeks of."

King let a smirk pull at the corner of his mouth as he stood and adjusted the sleeves of his suit.

"Let's go let 'em know we ain't tourists."

The cabin door hissed open, and the heat hit like a brick wall humid, thick with salt, money, and blood.

Waiting by the SUV was Dominic "Dom" GrindTime King's son, the sports mogul turned nightlife and media king. Dom was sharp in linen, shades on, hair twisted back, and energy electric.

"Pops," Dom grinned, dapping his father. "You ready to own this playground?"

King nodded. "Only reason we came."

Vinnie tossed his duffel in the trunk. "So, Dom... tell me somethin'. What's the Vasquez boys been up to?"

Dom slid into the driver's seat of the armored black Escalade and tapped the screen.

"Overconfident. They are buying up clubs, casinos, even whispering' in politicians' ears. Think they are running shit."

King leaned back, letting the AC hit him. "Good. That means they got something to lose."

As the SUV rolled through the city, they passed the glowing strip of Ocean Drive music blaring from open-air bars, models laughing under neon signs, Lambos parked like status trophies.

But King wasn't impressed.

He was scouting.

Miami was beautiful. But beautiful things were usually built on ugly foundations. And those cracks? That's where King did his best work.

Big Ty watched a street dealer hand something off to a tourist. "You see that?"

King nodded. "They got reach. But not structure."

Dom smirked. "They are sloppy. Fast money, loud moves, too many faces."

King cracked his knuckles. "We fix that. By replacing 'em."

Vinnie's phone buzzed. He scanned the message, then whistled low.

"La Luna. That's were Vasquez's people at tonight. VIP heavy. Security real cute."

King tapped his ring against the window.

"No statements. No threats. We walk in like we own it because after tonight, we will."

Big Ty chuckled. "That's the King I know."

Minutes later, the Escalade slowed in front of La Luna Club a towering, all-white fortress of luxury and vice. Blue velvet ropes. Palm trees swaying like they knew trouble just pulled up.

Security stepped forward six-deep, tactical vests, sidearms showing.

One of them squared his shoulders. “This a private event tonight”

King stepped out of the SUV, slow, deliberate.

His watch gleamed. His presence froze time.

He didn’t raise his voice. He didn’t have to.

“Tell your boss... King GrindTime’s here.”

The security guard hesitated. He looked at the others.

Vinnie sighed and stepped forward.

“He said tell your boss. Before I teach you what time it is.”

The guard scrambled back, hand on his earpiece, whispering fast.

The velvet ropes of La Luna’s VIP section parted like the Red Sea.

Chapter Five

Welcome to Miami

King GrindTime walked through first slow, surgical, silent. The club's beat pulsed around him, but it might as well have been quiet. That's the kind of presence he carried.

Behind him, Vinnie peeled off his shades, eyes darting counting exits, scanning threats, clocking faces. He leaned in close, voice low.

"Three goons. One behind Vasquez, two posted near the DJ booth. All strapped. I can smell the gun oil."

Big Ty followed last, large, unbothered, chewing on a toothpick like he was strolling into a cookout. But the subtle shift in his gait? That was war walk.

Miguel Vasquez remained seated in his booth. He didn't stand. Didn't flinch. Just raised his glass slowly and sipped his dark rum like he didn't just step into his own execution.

"King GrindTime," he said with a smug grin. "Didn't think you'd show up so... personally."

King didn't sit. Not yet.

He stared for a moment long enough to let the silence crawl across Miguel's skin.

"So..." Miguel said, drawing it out.

"The man who walks like a legend.

They said you'd never leave Ohio."

King's eyes didn't move.

"Legends move in silence.

Until they have to be loud."

Miguel chuckled.

"Still slick with the talk.

But this is Miami, Papi.

We don't move on words.

We move on blood."

King leaned in, his voice calm, but heavy.

"And I build empires off both."

The two stood face to face. Here stood generations of power clashing silently in front of the city's high society.

Champagne froze mid-glass.

Even the dancers paused.

Miguel gestured to a nearby booth.

"Let's talk, yeah?

Maybe this doesn't have to turn messy."

King nodded once.

"We talk. But

You don't leave this conversation the same."

Then he sat.

"I make it a habit to show up when I'm taking something."

Miguel's grin twitched. "Miami's a long way from Ohio."

King smirked. "I've already been through New York, Cleveland, Atlanta, Philly. Everywhere I land becomes mine. Miami's just the latest."

Miguel chuckled, leaning back like he wasn't being sized for a casket.

"You really think you can walk into my city, my turf, and play king?"

King raised a hand.

"No. I don't play king. I am king. You just been living in the throne I built years ago."

The air between them tightened.

Vasquez's hand hovered near his drink, but his eyes were watching King's every twitch. The women with him instantly quiet. Even the security behind him looked unsure.

King leaned in, elbows on the table, voice ice-cold.

"I'm here to give you a choice."

Miguel raised an eyebrow. "A choice?"

King's tone dropped even lower.

"Business... or blood."

Miguel scoffed. "You think I don't see what this is? A threat?"

"No," King said, smiling calmly. "A promise."

Vinnie stepped forward slightly. Not enough to cause alarm just enough to remind every soul in that room who the real threat was.

Miguel's jaw tightened. He looked at the club around them, at the life he'd built on bluff and bravado, and for the first time... he looked unsure.

"You walk in here, into my place, like you already own it"

"I do," King interrupted. "Half your coke supply routes are mine now. Your clean money? Being funneled through shell companies I control. Your politicians? Already took my calls."

Miguel sat across, flanked by his men.

"So, tell me," Miguel said, swirling his drink,

"Why Miami?

You already run half the Midwest.

Stay in your lane."

King leaned back, eyes locked.

"Your lane's flooded.

Weak structure.

Greedy soldiers.

Clubs leaking' coke, girls, and cash out the back doors.

You don't even know who's stealing from you."

Miguel's jaw twitched.

"Watch your mouth."

King flicked ashes onto the silver tray.

"I am. But I ain't watching my moves.

Your city's cracking.

I'm here to offer reinforcement. Or replacement."

Vinnie slid a black leather folder across the table.

Dom tapped it.

"That's a full audit of your empire.

Including three of your closest people

funneling product to Puerto Rican cartels

behind your back."

Miguel hesitated.

His bravado cracked for half a second.

"You're lying."

King didn't blink.

"Check page six."

Miguel opened it.

Flipped.

Saw names. Photos. Wire transfers.

Security cam stills.

His fingers tightened around the glass.

King leaned in.

"This ain't personal.

It's protection.

Your enemies are in your house.

And if I don't clean it up...

somebody else will.

You just won't live to see it."

Miguel looked between King and his crew.

"You really think you can come into my city

and run things?"

King stood up.

"Correction.

I don't think.

I know."

As he turned to leave, King dropped a black envelope onto the table.

“In there is my proposal.

Two choices.

Join us...

or get buried with what’s left of your empire.”

Miguel opened the envelope.

Inside was a single bullet...

and a card.

GrindTime Holdings.

Miami Division.

Coming Soon.

Miguel’s face went pale for a flash of a second. Then he masked it with anger.

“You think that makes you untouchable?”

King stood, buttoning his jacket.

“No. That makes you disposable.”

He turned to walk away.

Miguel raised his voice. “What if I say no?”

King paused. Looked over his shoulder, eyes glinting with something primal.

“Then I bury you so deep, your ancestors gonna suffocate.”

Vinnie grinned wide. Big Ty just nodded once, slow and sure.

As the trio walked out of the VIP, silence followed them like a shadow. Eyes tracked their every step. Miguel sat frozen, glass trembling slightly in his hand.

Because deep down, he knew

This wasn’t a deal.

It was a death sentence with a 24-hour grace period.

Chapter Six

Business Or Blood

The ice in Miguel Vasquez's glass clinked softly, the only sound in the dim VIP lounge as La Luna's thumping bass faded behind soundproof glass. He stared into the dark amber of his rum like it could offer him divine guidance.

It didn't. His world the empire he built had just been put on notice. Across from him sat Ramon Diaz, his second in-command.

Younger, colder, trigger-happy.

Ramon was the type to solve problems with bullets before asking questions.

He had a scar running from his jaw to his collarbone which was a gift from a failed coup years ago.

"Boss," Ramon said, his tone urgent. "We strike now. That's our only play."

Miguel didn't move. Didn't even blink. He just whispered, "He already owns half of me."

Ramon leaned forward, eyes blazing. "Then let's take back the other half. We got soldiers. Firepower. Connections. Let's remind King GrindTime who built this city."

Miguel finally looked up. His eyes weren't angry.

They were calculating.

"No, Hermano. King didn't come here to negotiate. That man came to take over. And that means he already moved his pieces."

He turned slowly, glancing toward the bar. Two of his guards were already gone. The bartender is King's guy. The DJ is King's guy. He felt it now, like a chill crawling up his spine.

Ramon didn't get it. "So, what, we just bow down? Let him stomp on us?"

"No," Miguel said. He set the glass down and stood slowly, straightening his blazer. "We find out how deep he's cut into my operation. Every leak. Every double agent. Every dollar that disappeared. I want it all. Tonight."

Ramon nodded and rushed out the room.

Miguel stood alone for a beat longer, then whispered to himself:

"You want war, King?"

He looked out over the neon-drenched city that once knelt to him.

"Then bleed for it."

He didn't sleep that night.

None of them did.

Because when power is threatened, it doesn't retreat.

It prepares to kill. And that night? Miami held its breath.

Chapter Seven

The Longest Night

The GrindTime Miami Estate wasn't a mansion it was a fortress dressed in luxury. Marble floors gleamed like water. High ceilings echoed every footstep. Outside, armed guards moved like shadows. Inside, the war room was alive.

King GrindTime sat low in a leather chair, sipping from a glass of black rum and letting the weed roll through his system like medicine. The silence in the room wasn't awkward it was strategy.

Dom paced near the floor-to-ceiling windows overlooking the palm lined driveway. "Pops," he said, voice sharp with tension, "Vasquez ain't going to roll over. You know that, right?"

King gave a slight smirk. "I'd be insulted if he did."

Big Ty sat slouched on the couch, arms crossed, eyes locked on the TV playing an old Western. "He's coming hard. He got too much pride to let you just take the city."

Vinnie stood behind the bar, cleaning a chrome-plated Desert Eagle with surgical precision. "He's already tried. Sent two hitters to tail me from the club last night. Didn't make it past the causeway."

King nodded slightly. "Good. That means he's moving scared."

Just then, the thick oak doors opened.

Mama GrindTime entered like the air changed for her.

Her silver braids were wrapped high, her long coat brushing the marble floor, and in her hand.

A carved ebony cane that held more stories than most men had years. She didn't need a gun. Her eyes were weapons enough.

"Boy," she said calmly, staring dead at King, "you ready for this war?"

King rose, meeting her gaze without flinching. "Always."

She stepped into the room like a priestess entering sacred ground.

"Then let me tell you what you already know. Vasquez is gonna hit first. He ain't built to sit back and think."

Vinnie chuckled. "That's what makes him sloppy."

Mama ignored the interruption.

"You think he's for you. But he's coming for your legacy. Your name. Your reach. He doesn't want your blood. He wants your reputation dead."

King took a deep breath, letting her words soak in. "Then we show him what a legend bleeds like."

She raised her cane and pointed it at him. "Make sure when you hit back, there ain't a damn soul left to hold his crown."

Dom whistled low under his breath.

Big Ty stood, cracking his knuckles. "It's time, huh?"

King set down his drink and turned toward his generals. "Ty gets our people on alert. Lock the city from the inside out. Dom, I want visuals on every movement Vasquez makes. Vinnie..."

"I already know," Vinnie said, loading a fresh clip.

"Let him think he's got the drop. Then bury his whole bloodline."

Mama GrindTime gave a quiet, approving nod.

"Then go ahead, baby. Show the world what happens when they pick a fight with the pressure."

"RoyaL Blood Never Fades"

Chapter Eight

When You're the Threat

News spread faster than bullets.

Two days passed.

Twenty-four hours of silence in Miami

that felt louder than a warzone.

Whispers filled the clubs.

Dealers started switching allegiances.

Gun runners paused their deliveries.

And the city held its breath.

King wasn't worried.

He'd seen this before; that quiet before an empire cracks.

But this time, he wasn't defending one.

He was taking it.

In a hidden warehouse off 27th Avenue,

King's new Miami command post was alive.

Flat screens mapped every known drug route.

Photos of cartel lieutenants were pinned to cork boards.

Stacks of burner phones rang and were tossed out just as fast.

Cash counters hummed like lullabies.

Serenity's face flashed across one of the monitors a video call home.

King stepped into the side office and smiled.

"Hey, baby girl."

She grinned, laughing hysterically

"Daddy! I showed Mama how to play Spades, and I WON!"

He laughed.

"You hustling' already?"

She nodded.

"I'm like you.

I won't lose."

His eyes softened.

"You're right. Stay winning."

Serenity leaned closer to the camera.

"Are you being safe?"

King paused.

"Always.

I got angels with me."

She smiled, blew a kiss, said I love you and the screen went dark.

King GrindTime and his top men were expected to appear at Club DeLuxe tonight, the crown jewel of Miami nightlife.

To outsiders, it looked like arrogance.

To insiders, it was bait.

The night was humid enough to make a palm tree sweat.

Bright lights flashed from the club's front like paparazzi on crack. The line wrapped around the building, filled with influencers, hustlers, and fake rich posing for validation.

But when King pulled up in a matte black bulletproof SUV, the energy shifted.

He stepped out in a midnight-blue tailored suit with gold threaded lapels.

His chain shimmered.

His eyes didn't.

Vinnie followed behind in an all-black trench and matching gloves looking more like a ghost than a man.

Big Ty had on camo cargo pants and a blood-red hoodie with "LOYALTY" stitched across the chest.

His gold tooth flashed with every smirk.

Security stepped aside without a word.

Cameras dropped.

Everyone recognized royalty.

Inside, the bass pulsed through every wall, the scent of designer cologne, liquor, and sex saturating the air. Models in VIP danced on couches. Athletes and execs pretended not to notice King, but everyone noticed.

They made their way to the VIP booth overlooking the club floor. King lit a blunt. "Now we wait."

"Think he bites?" Big Ty asked.

"He already did," Vinnie answered, eyes scanning the exits. "I left him crumbs. He's starving."

Fifteen minutes later, the door near the back creaked open.

Ramon Diaz entered.

Miguel Vasquez's second-in-command. Slim suit. Snake eyes. Five men flanking him armed, clearly nervous.

King didn't move.

Vinnie's hand rested on his thigh holster. Big Ty stood up slow, like stretching before a workout.

Ramon approached the booth with a swagger that didn't match the fear in his scent.

"My boss sends his regards," he said, voice tense.

King exhaled a cloud of smoke. “He should’ve sent a priest.”

Ramon flinched slightly. “He’s got a counteroffer for you.”

King’s smile was razor thin. “We don’t do counteroffers.”

Ramon reached into his jacket pocket

That’s when Vinnie moved.

BOOM.

One clean shot.

Ramon dropped like dead weight; blood splattered across the bottle of Ace of Spades.

Screams. Panic. The club turned into a stampede.

Big Ty calmly wiped blood off his hoodie. “Guess that answers that.”

King stood, stepped over Ramon’s body, and took one final puff from his blunt.

A single shot shattered the night.

Time slowed.

Ramon’s body jerked backward, arms flailing like a puppet with cut strings. His back slammed against the velvet booth, eyes frozen wide in disbelief. The bullet tore through his chest, spraying blood across the table like spilled wine at a cursed communion.

Vinnie lowered his gun, still warm, smoke curling from the barrel. “I told you not to reach, bitch.”

Chaos exploded.

Screams erupted from every direction. Glass shattered. Bottles dropped. The crowd panicked, stampeding toward the exits. Security scrambled, drawing weapons, shouting into earpieces.

King GrindTime calmly plucking a fresh blunt from his coat pocket.

Big Ty grabbed one of the panicked guards trying to flee past the booth and slammed him face-first into the marble floor.

“Wrong fuckin’ party.”

More guards drew their weapons but saw Vinnie pointing both Glocks their way, eyes wild with joy.

“Try it,” he whispered.

The club’s staff vanished. The lights dimmed. All that remained were echoes of the music, the fading smoke from Vinnie’s shot, and Ramon’s body slumped across the booth like a broken offering.

King stood slowly, adjusting the cuffs of his suit with deliberate elegance. “We just declared war.”

Big Ty tossed a bloody napkin onto Ramon’s corpse. “Guess there goes negotiations.”

Vinnie holstered one of his guns and laughed. “We came in for a drink, walked out with a body count. This place got five stars on Yelp?”

King turned toward the exit, nodding once to his team. “Clean up our trail. Make sure everyone in here forgets what they saw or forgets how to breathe.”

Big Ty smirked. “On it.”

Vinnie looked down at Ramon’s body, then leaned in and whispered, “Tell Miguel we’re coming.”

The booth drenched in blood, the scent of death clinging to the cushions like cigar smoke. Outside, the Miami sky cracked with thunder, no rain, just tension. The kind that dripped from every rooftop and soaked into the bones of the city.

As they walked out, sirens wailed in the distance. But none of them looked back.

Because this wasn’t the beginning of the war. This was the cost of disrespect and the GrindTime Familia had just paid it in full.

Vinnie cracked his neck, sliding his weapon back into its holster. “So... what’s the next move?”

King looked out over the chaos like a king watching ant's scatter.

“We burn Vasquez’s empire to the ground.”

All three of them locked eyes, smirking in unison.

“Let the fire begin.”

"Only Truth Survives The War"

Chapter Nine

Setting the Trap

The air in the warehouse had shifted.

Even before Vinnie spoke, King could feel it

that eerie vibration that rides in just before chaos knocks.

Vinnie's boots echoed as he approached from the shadows,

jaw clenched, a vein pulsing at his temple.

He didn't speak right away.

Just stood in front of King, breathing through rage.

"They moved."

King didn't blink. He simply looked up from the glass of Tequila in his hand.

"Who?"

Vinnie's eyes locked in. No hesitation.

"Miguel.

They hit the Dominican ports. Last night.

He intercepted our shipment...

The containers are gone.

He burned it all."

Then Vinnie reached into his coat, pulled out a half-scorched piece of paper.

Charred around the edges.

Still warm from hate.

"No Kings in MY city."

King took the paper, held it to the light.

The bold marker ink still dripped, smudged from heat and arrogance.

Across the room, Big Ty was already on his feet.

He snatched the note, nostrils flaring.

"Oh, he's disrespectful.

Fucking penguin-built cornball.

Wanna play games?"

Dom, who'd been silent in the corner cleaning rifles, calmly started loading clips, his movements clean, methodical, the way a soldier readies for war without wasting words.

The Calm Before the Blood

King stood, slow and deliberate.

He walked to the center of the room, boots clicking on concrete, eyes scanning the war board covered in maps, names, ports, routes, and red lines.

He didn't yell.

Didn't flinch.

Didn't blink.

He just dropped the note to the ground.

Then came the words that made everyone in the room tighten their grip on reality: "Send the wave."

The Streets Answer

The retaliation wasn't loud.

Not at first.

It was calculated.

At exactly 2:13 AM, four separate GrindTime crews moved like whispers through the streets of Little Havana, Overtown, and Brickell.

By 2:34, two of Miguel's prized stash houses had gone up in flames.

The kind of flames that sent black smoke clawing into the Miami night sky.

At 2:46, a third location was breached.

GrindTime soldiers didn't just burn the work

they left behind bags of fake powder

cut with poison, so if Miguel's re-up still touched the streets, he'd be killing his own customers.

At 3:02 AM, two bodies were pulled from Biscayne Bay.

Faces unrecognizable.

Hands zip-tied.

Cinder blocks chained to their ankles.

One had a GrindTime coin shoved into his mouth.

Now it was time for the Clubs to fold.

The GrindTime intel squad had already infiltrated Miguel's nightlife.

Club security was Flipped.

Promoters?

Bought off.

The dancers?

Already on GrindTime payroll for months feeding info, tracking movements, planting bugs.

The GrindTime Familia was moving like the Mob, BMF, Cartels, Community leaders and the damn D.E.A all wrapped in one.

The clubs were hit with coordinated raids, but not by the police.

No, this was surgical.

Rooms swept.

Hard drives snatched.

Cash drawers emptied.

By the time the sun kissed the water,

Miguel's reputation was bleeding in the gutters of South Beach.

There was no place to run for Miguel.

His team was being chewed up piece by piece and his infrastructure was being demolished dollar by dollar.

And now every kingpin within 500 miles knows what happens when you test this bloodline."

He turned slowly, his crown pendant glinting under the light.

"We don't just rule. We teach."

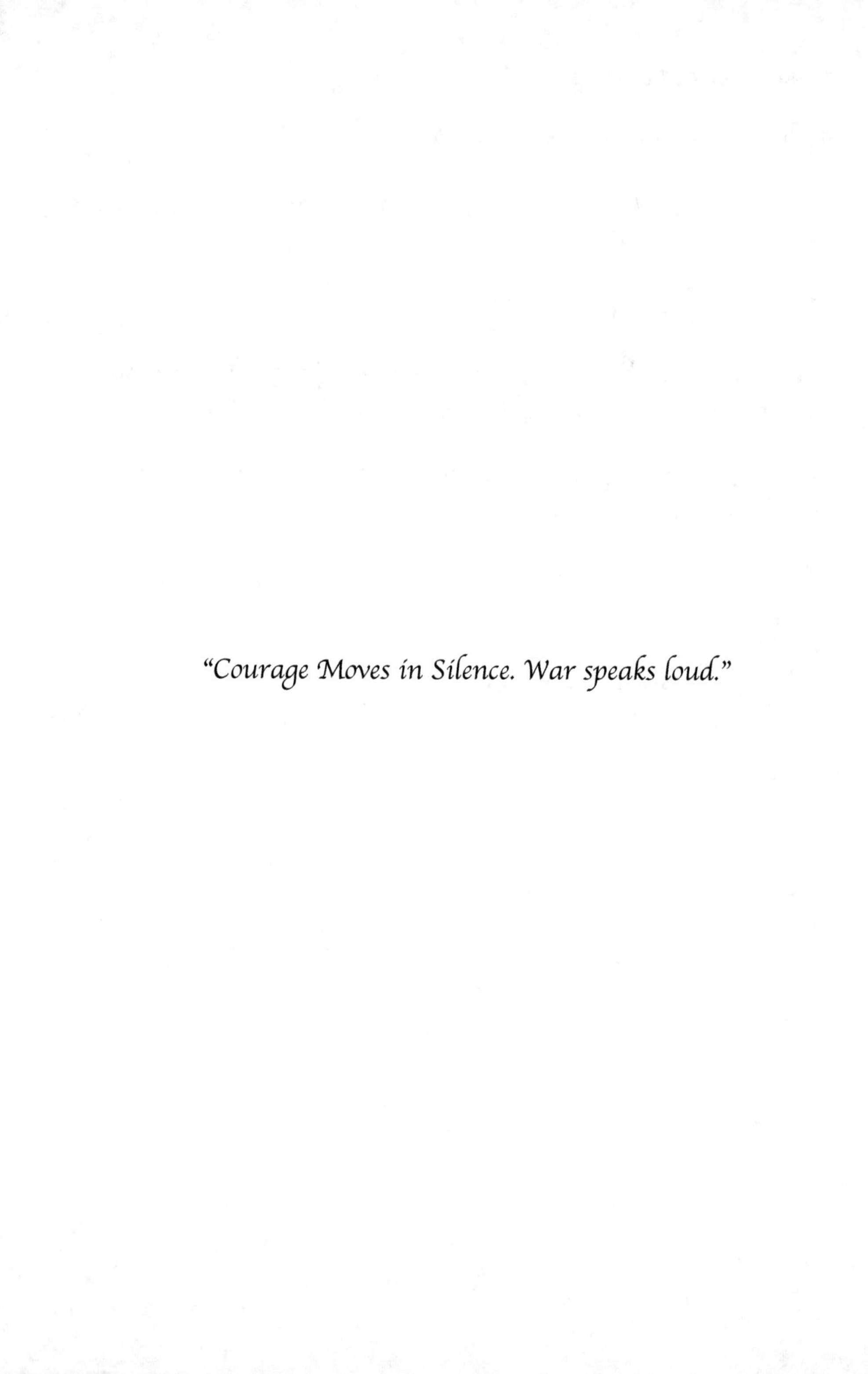

"Courage Moves in Silence. War speaks loud."

Chapter Ten

The Price of War

The Miami night air was thick with decisions, smoke, and vengeance. From the rooftop of a high-rise overlooking the city's glittering coastline, King GrindTime stood in silence, a blunt smoldering between his fingers. His gold rings shimmered in the glow of distant fire three separate explosions now lit the Miami skyline like twisted fireworks.

Down below, chaos reigned.

Sirens howled.

Helicopters cut across the sky.

And three of Miguel Vasquez's key distribution warehouses strategically located in Wynwood, Opa-locka, and Little Havana were now engulfed in violent, roaring flame.

King didn't flinch.

He simply inhaled.

Exhaled.

Vinnie stepped beside him, wiping black soot off his leather jacket. "Warehouse three went up better than planned. Shit looked like a Denzel Washington flick," he said, grinning. "Ty's crew rigged that gas line perfect."

King's eyes remained fixed on the inferno. "How many casualties?"

"Only Vasquez's side. We cleared all civilians. We not them."

King nodded once, slow. Intentional. "Good. Then they'll know this wasn't a message... it was a promise."

Across the rooftop, Big Ty emerged from the stairwell, still catching his breath, vest unzipped, shirt damp with sweat.

"All three sites down. Miami ain't gonna sleep for the next two weeks. D.E.A gon' have heart attacks tryna figure out who moved like this."

King turned from the edge, walking into the makeshift war room they had set up at the top of the high-rise. Maps lined the walls. Surveillance footage streamed on tablets and laptops. Dom, Jules, and Ava were already in motion each coordinating their divisions from different floors of the building.

A secure phone vibrated. Jules answered, then passed it to King.

On the line: Miguel Vasquez.

His voice was shaky low and filled with venom.

"You think you can do this to me? You think you can walk into my city, burn my empire, and just fly away untouched?"

King's voice was ice. "I didn't walk in. I took it."

“You’ll regret this,” Vasquez snarled. “You want Miami? You’ll have to bleed for every block!”

King let the silence settle for a moment. Then he said flatly, “That was always the plan.”

He hung up.

Big Ty chuckled from the corner, flipping a gold coin between his fingers. “I think he gon’ bleed harder than us.”

Vinnie sat back in a leather chair, reloading his Glock.

“His supply lines gone. His men scattered. And the streets? They talkin’. They sayin’ Vasquez ain’t even the top dog no more.”

King grabbed a backwood from the cigar box on the table. He lit it, letting the flame dance for a moment too long before he pulled. “He’s not. We are.”

Ava’s voice buzzed through the intercom. “Press coverage on firebombings already spinning. Our media contacts are flooding headlines with cartel infighting theories. They won’t trace it back to us.”

Jules added, “And I just rerouted three shell accounts of Vasquez’s own money. Paid for the damn explosions with his own blood money.”

King cracked a smile. “Poetic.”

A pause fell over the room.

Then King walked over to a glass case in the corner inside was a black book, leather-bound, with a GrindTime crest engraved in gold.

He opened it and began writing.

Vinnie glanced over his shoulder. “What’s that brother?”

King didn’t look up. “The death ledger. Every man that tried us goes in here. One day, Serenity’s kids will read it and know this didn’t come easy. It came with real blood, pain, and faith. We had to be smart, dedicated and sacrifice to make the world we live in today better for our people tomorrow.”

Three single explosions simultaneously echoed louder than 100 fireworks show grand finales all lighting their fireworks at once.

Each warehouse collapsed completely, sending a shockwave through the city.

Car alarms blared.

Dogs barked.

Sirens sounded.

Helicopters swarmed.

But in that rooftop war room, GrindTime stood calm.

Because this wasn’t chaos.

It was control.

King snapped the ledger shut.

“Let Vasquez call his people if the fucking pig still has any people left.

“Let him beg the crooked cops they will get exposed and put in the dirt right next to him to if he fucks around.”

“Let him whine to all of his little politicians every single one will get exposed for the illegal and weird shit they are into.”

Big Ty leaned against the window, watching the flames.

“He gon’ realize quickly...” he muttered.

King finished the thought:

“You don’t negotiate with God's gifts.”

" Royal Blood, dirty hands, clean heart."

Chapter Eleven

Midnight Fire

Back in Columbus, Ohio.

The wind outside Mama GrindTime's old two-story home howled like it carried the voices of the dead whispers of soldiers, ghosts of those who had once pledged loyalty but fell to ego, bullets, or betrayal.

It was a cool, gray evening of those days where the weather makes your bones ache and memories crawl out from between the cracks in old walls a little.

She sat in that same weathered wooden chair she had claimed for decades.

The one that creaked like it had secrets.

A faded quilt draped over her lap.

Her fingers scarred, ringed, and steadily moving over the deck of tarot cards like she was shuffling war plans.

The room was quiet, save for the slow drag of breath and the occasional crackle of the fireplace, where flames danced like spirits daring to be seen.

She didn't often put faith in superstition.

Not the kind found in books or on late-night TV.

But this?

This was different.

This was blood-line deep.

The ancestors didn't whisper through incense; they spoke through intuition, and tonight they were loud.

She flipped a card.

The Tower.

A violent upheaval. Chaos. Collapse.

Another card.

Judgement.

Reckoning. A call from the higher realm. Truth, no matter how bloody.

She paused, exhaled through her nose, and reached for the burner phone beside her crystal ashtray.

Typed one message.

> "Don't let your enemies choose the battleground.
> You pick it... or they bury you on theirs."

She hit send, then stared into the fire like it owed her an explanation.

Thousands of Miles Away in the Atlantic Waters.

The GrindTime yacht sliced through the sea with purpose.

It wasn't flashy like most kingpins would use.

It was armored. Silent. Smooth.

Built more for war than for leisure.

More of a submarine than a boat.

Under the deck was a mobile command room.

Above deck was, King who stood silent observing the hidden secrets of the world through each wave passing with the blunt lit.

Smoke curled around his face as he stared across the open water, where hours earlier Biscayne Bay had exploded into chaos leaving stash houses crumbling, men floating, clubs cracked wide open like rotten fruit.

But this silence?

It wasn't a victory.

It was the warning that always came before the real war.

Behind him, Big Ty paced slowly, knuckles raw, blood still under his fingernails.

Vinnie leaned on the railing, counting ships on the horizon like he was reading Morse code in waves.

"Miami's shook," Vinnie muttered.

"But Miguel ain't the only snake left in the grass."

King didn't answer immediately.

He was still replaying his mother's words,

letting them echo like war drums inside his mind.

You pick the battleground... or they bury you on theirs.

The real threat wasn't just revenge.

It was a misdirection.

Enemies were bleeding now, yes.

But they were also watching.

Regrouping.

Plotting.

Back at Mama GrindTime's House the next morning, Mama GrindTime was in the garden now, despite the wind tending to her collard greens and herbs like it was still 1996.

Her sister, Auntie May, watched from the porch, arms crossed.

"You really think he ready for what's comin'?" she asked.

Mama didn't look up.

"Baby... he was born in the storm.

All I did was teach him how to dance in it."

As Nightfall approached

King sat alone in the command deck's war room.

Screens lit with surveillance.

Messages from allies and spies.

Three enemies were circled.

Two were marked for elimination.

One?

Still hiding.

He leaned forward, eyes steady.

Voice like thunder crawling up from hell.

“Tomorrow, we move first.

No more reaction.

No more waiting.

No more mercy.”

Big Ty walked in, cleaning his blade.

“What’s the target?”

King stood.

Walked over to a steel cabinet.

Opened it.

Inside: maps, black files, and an old-school switchblade from his childhood days.

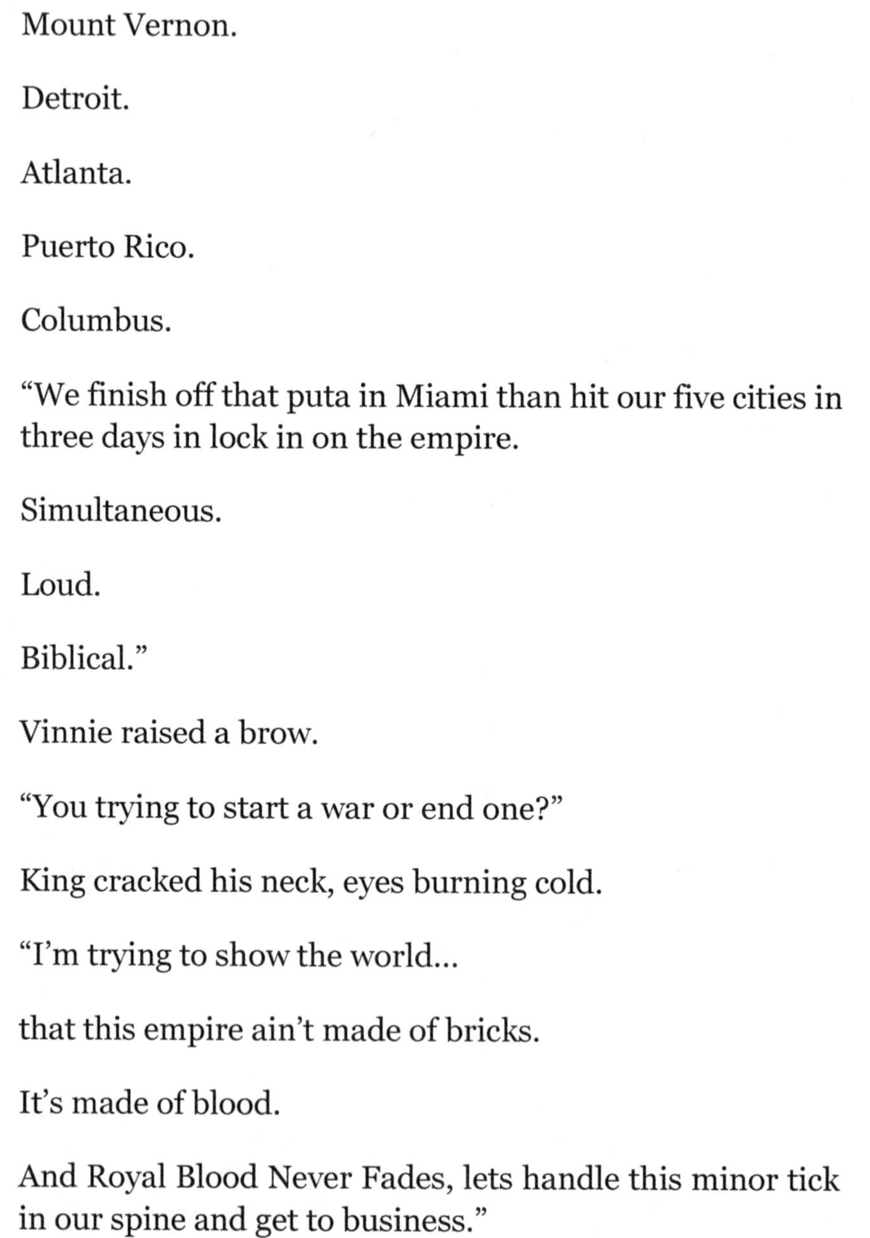

He placed the blade on the table and pointed to a red marked zone:

Yonkers.

Mount Vernon.

Detroit.

Atlanta.

Puerto Rico.

Columbus.

“We finish off that puta in Miami than hit our five cities in three days in lock in on the empire.

Simultaneous.

Loud.

Biblical.”

Vinnie raised a brow.

“You trying to start a war or end one?”

King cracked his neck, eyes burning cold.

“I’m trying to show the world...

that this empire ain’t made of bricks.

It’s made of blood.

And Royal Blood Never Fades, lets handle this minor tick in our spine and get to business.”

Chapter Twelve:

The Storm Before the Execution

Deep in the high hills of Miami's outskirts, where palm trees gave way to wrought-iron fences and private security outnumbered the police, Miguel Vasquez sat in the belly of his empire: a sprawling mansion built like a fortress.

Floodlights scanned the tree lines. Helicopter blades echoed overhead. Fifty men with rifles patrolled the grounds like war dogs. Inside, Miguel paced his study, downing glass after glass of dark rum, hands trembling.

He had ruled Miami with an iron grip for over a decade. But now? In the span of forty-eight hours, his supply lines were torched, his lieutenants slaughtered, and his name carried no weight in the streets.

King GrindTime had come for him. Not with questions. Not with negotiations.

With fire.

Chavez Diaz, Vasquez last remaining capo, entered the study, face slick with sweat. "Boss. We got three black SUVs approaching the front gate. Fast."

Vasquez grabbed his rifle and loaded it with a clack. "Is it him?"

"Looks like it."

"Then we die fighting."

Outside, King's convoy pulled up like a funeral procession for an empire.

Big Ty drove the lead SUV, engine rumbling like a beast caged too long. Vinnie rode shotgun, eyes scanning through night vision. Behind them, twenty elite shooters dressed in black and moving with cold precision stepped into position.

King lit a blunt and stepped out of the second SUV, his custom pistol gleaming under the moonlight.

"Go loud," he said.

Ty grinned, then rammed the gates at full speed. Metal crumpled like tissue.

Explosions followed charges Vinnie had planted earlier lit up the mansion's perimeter like fireworks on Judgment Day. Gunfire erupted from every direction.

Ty led the front-line assault, moving like a wrecking ball through concrete and bone. Vinnie took the flanks, his silencer barking death in shadows.

GrindTime's soldiers moved through the estate with military discipline, cutting down Vasquez's forces floor by floor.

And King?

He walked straight through the front door.

Inside, Miguel Vasquez stood in his study, rifle in hand. The smell of sweat and gun oil filled the air.

King entered without a word.

Miguel aimed, finger twitching but he was too slow.

Two shots.

One to the knee. One to the shoulder.

He dropped, screaming.

King approached slowly, crouching beside him, face unreadable.

“You had a choice,” King said. “Business or blood. You chose pride so I chose blood.”

Miguel snarled through gritted teeth. “You ain’t no king. You are just another thug.”

King smiled. “Then you just got dethroned by a thug.”

He stood.

Big Ty and Vinnie dragged Vasquez out, bleeding and broken.

“What we do with him?” Ty asked.

King looked out over the mansion, smoke curling in the hallways. Then, he said:

“Strip him of everything. Tie him up. Put him on a boat. Push him out to sea.”

Vinnie blinked. “Let him live?”

“Shoot holes in both his hands and feet. If he makes it back, he can keep whatever he finds.

We already burned his empire, and the mother fucker don't got no feet no more."

As Vasquez was dragged out, moaning in pain, King turned back to the fireplace and tossed a stack of cash inside.

The flames rose higher.

Chapter Thirteen:

Vasquez's Last Stand

Morning bled across Miami like a bruised eye swelling open.

The skyline shimmered under a haze of smoke and salt.

Ash drifted lazily through the air like ghostly confetti tossed after a funeral nobody wanted to attend but everybody knew was necessary.

Helicopters buzzed overhead like metal vultures.

News vans choked the avenues.

Reporters shouted theories into cameras, battling for the best shot outside smoldering warehouses and boarded-up clubs.

But in the streets?

The truth had already whispered its way through every block, barber shop, and bodega.

Vasquez was gone.

And a new king had claimed his throne.

The Rise of the Family Continues

Dom GrindTime didn't ask permission.

He moved in like a shadow swallowing light one club at a time.

By nightfall, his face was already stamped on every VIP list, and the old security crews had been replaced with soldiers rocking GrindTime rings under their gloves.

Casinos, strip lounges, bottle-service, night life entertainment was not just taken.

They were remodeled, rebranded, reborn.

Dom didn't just own the night he became the night.

Velvet ropes parted when he stepped in.

DJs stopped their sets to salute him.

The women?

They didn't just dance for the room.

They danced for the dynasty.

Meanwhile, Jules GrindTime sank beneath the surface like a well-fed shark.

While chaos burned above, he moved silently through the financial underworld, sealing deals with offshore bank managers, routing old Vasquez capital through Belize, Panama, Dubai, and back again through Miami real estate.

No loose ends.

No dirty trails.

No holes in the vault.

In one week, Jules acquired two small banks, a cryptocurrency firm, and a silent stake in the largest construction company in Dade County.

He didn't wear crowns.

He wore paper.

Ava GrindTime stepped into the spotlight like a phoenix wrapped in designer flame.

She rebranded the GrindTime name with a vision that bled across music, fashion, cannabis, media, and culture.

Her first move?

An exclusive launch party in Wynwood featuring unreleased tracks, fashion collabs with underground designers, and influencers dripping in her newest scent. A weed-scented cologne called "Loyalty."

The smell alone was intoxicating.

Earthy. Forbidden. Addictive.

By the end of the night, her face was on five magazine covers, and her brand had trended across every corner of social media.

GrindTime wasn't just in the streets anymore.

It was in every phone, feed, and playlist.

Gabi GrindTime was never loud because real control doesn't make noise.

She wore suits like armor and carried herself with a courtroom chill.

And in under 72 hours, she made sure:

- Three judges owed her favors.
- Two zoning boards passed emergency permits.
- One state senator was on her personal line.

Every piece of red tape tied itself into a bow the moment she walked into a room.

You didn't see her coming.

But if you crossed her?

You'd feel the weight of the law bury your entire bloodline.

Then there was Serenity. The glue that kept the siblings together.

She wasn't just the future.

She was the one King trusted with the heartbeat of everything.

While the others rebuilt the empire's bones, Serenity shaped its soul crafting digital campaigns, running outreach programs, and connecting with the young voices often overlooked by empires obsessed with wealth and warfare.

She rolled out branded education platforms.

Mental health outreach.

Streetwear lines for teens and kids.

Animation series that told their story through new lenses.

She didn't wait for a seat at the table.

She built her own table that will keep GrindTime living forever, then taught the next generation how to eat.

King GrindTime stood on the balcony, blunt burning slowly between his fingers in the penthouse suite that once belonged to Vasquez, a glass fortress that stared down at Miami like it was prey.

The ocean stretched beyond him symbolizing endless opportunities, possibilities, violence, peace and life colliding together.

Each wave crashing below was a reminder:

Power moves like water.

And he had just redirected the current.

Behind him, the room was silent.

No music.

No noise.

Just the muffled sound of power breathing.

Then his phone buzzed.

He answered without looking.

Mama GrindTime.

Her voice came through like gravel and gospel.

"You done?" she asked, no warmth in her tone.

King exhaled, letting the smoke curl skyward.

"Miami is ours."

There was a long pause.

Then Mama's voice dropped into that ancestral octave the kind forged from generations of pain, prophecy, and purpose.

"Good," she said.
"Now get ready for the real war."

King stared back at the sea.

A grin crept slowly across his lips.

"I was hoping you'd say that."

Because this?

This was just territory.

Power was global.

And GrindTime was just getting started.

Chapter Fourteen:

The New King of Miami

The Miami air was thick with victory, but King GrindTime knew better than to celebrate too early. From the balcony of the mansion that once belonged to Miguel Vasquez, he watched the waves roll in, his blunt burning slow in his hand. The city now bent to his will. Clubs, real estate, politicians he owned it all.

But true kings never got comfortable. Especially not with blood still drying in the streets.

Inside the mansion, Serenity, Dom, Ava, Jules, and Gabi were gathered in the newly christened war room. Screens displayed surveillance feeds from every corner of the empire Puerto Rico, Cleveland, Detroit, L.A., Atlanta, West Virgina, the Carolinas, Yonkers, and Columbus. The empire stretched far and wide. But power? Power brought enemies. And they were moving fast.

Mama GrindTime, always watching even from afar, sat on her porch back in Columbus. A thunderstorm cracked the sky as she rocked slowly, a perfectly rolled joint resting between her fingers like an old sword. Across from her sat a man she hadn't seen in years Detective Elijah Carter, the relentless force who had spent over a decade trying to bring King GrindTime down.

"You came all this way for what, Carter?" she asked, her voice calm, smoky, wrapped in the power of a woman who had outlived wars, betrayals, and revolutions.

Elijah leaned forward, the lines in his face deeper than the last time she saw him. “Your son thinks he’s untouchable.”

She chuckled, slow and measured. “That’s because he is.”

Elijah smirked, trying to conceal the fire behind his eyes. “Not for long.”

Mama GrindTime took a deep drag, exhaled toward the rain. “You spend too much time trying to stop a hurricane, you gon’ get swept up in it.”

Back in Miami, King paced the war room as reports flooded in.

“We got heat rising in Puerto Rico,” Jules said. “Some movement near the docks. Could be cartel remnants. Could be government contractors.”

“And what about the Streets in Columbus?” King asked, flicking ash into a crystal tray.

Ava chimed in, arms crossed, her eyes sharp as razors. “Whispers of a new task force being organized. A joint operation between the feds and local PD. Detective Carter's fingerprints are all over it.”

Big Ty entered the room, his massive frame filling the doorway. His shirt was stained with oil he’d just finished loading a new shipment himself. No job was too small when it came to protecting the kingdom.

“Brother,” Ty said, tossing a file onto the table. “One of our warehouses got raided in Cleveland. Real low-key. No news coverage. But our boy on the inside says it wasn’t regular police, it was military. Unmarked uniforms. Government-grade weapons."

King leaned forward, scanning the file. "How many did we lose?"

"Two dead. One missing. They took our heat, cash, and samples of our top-shelf strains," Ty answered.

King's eyes narrowed. "This ain't a coincidence."

Vinnie entered behind Ty, wiping grease off his hands. "I just got word. Somebody intercepted one of our encrypted deliveries. Vegas route. Same style quiet, clean, surgical."

King turned, gripping the edge of the table, the wood creaking under his fingers. "So, this is it. They are testing us on every front."

Gabi stood up, flipping her tablet toward the rest of the crew. "And now they're trying to pass federal legislation that would give the government full regulatory control over marijuana every grow site, every distributor, every lab."

"Which means they're coming for the Church," Ava said quietly.

King's eyes sharpened. "They don't realize they're already inside a storm."

Dom nodded. "We need to lock things down. Pull all top-level ops back into secured compounds. Send the warning GrindTime is on alert."

Mama GrindTime's voice rang in King's mind again:

"Power ain't just about what you build it's about how you hold it when the vultures start circling."

King stood straight, his decision made. "Nobody's circling this empire. We go on the offensive. If they want war? We give them a goddamn earthquake."

Everyone in the room froze for a second. Not in fear, but in clarity.

"Ty," King said, locking eyes with him. "Mobilize the guards in Cleveland, Columbus, and Puerto Rico. Fortify every block we own."

"Already done," Ty replied.

"Vinnie," King continued. "Set the birds to fly. I want eyes in every airspace above our territories. If the drone even thinks to move 10 blocks away, I wanna know."

"Consider it done," Vinnie said, cracking his knuckles.

"Gabi," King said, "I want every legal loophole dug up. Start pushing for immunity bills under the Church clause. Buy senators, flip judges, and make examples of anyone who tries to vote against us."

Gabi nodded. "They won't even see it coming."

Ava stepped forward. "And what about the press? They're going to spin this hard. Paint us as terrorists."

King turned toward her with a smile. "Then we become the heroes the people actually believe in. Please lock in with your little sister Serenity in put something together to make sure the people see the GrindTime way"

“Jules,” King said last. “Call the bankers. Liquidate thirty percent of our dormant funds. Start investing in survival infrastructure private hospitals, media networks, water plants. We ain’t just gonna ride this storm. We gon’ own it.”

Jules gave a single nod. “We’ll be recession-proof and revolution-ready.”

As the team dispersed, King stood alone in the room for a moment, the weight of war sitting on his shoulders like a crown made of steel. He reached into his coat, pulled out a small photo of an old shot of him, Serenity’s Mother, and their baby girl Serenity.

The foundation.

He closed his eyes, breathing in the moment.

They were coming.

But so was he.

And this time?

There would be no survivors.

" They whispered betrayal, I responded with a empire."

Chapter Fifteen

War on All Fronts

The jet never stopped moving.

The GrindTime Familia preferred it that way. Motion meant control. Stillness invited assassination.

The private Gulfstream cut through the night like a blade, engines humming low as the lights of the East Coast blurred beneath them.

Each city below was a chessboard.

Each stop was a reckoning.

King spoke to Vinnie and Ty as they sat on the private jet smoking their new strain of weed.

“Today, my brothers we must move quick, we just been hit again by some government knock offs again at a vital time in our organizations expansion.”

Yonkers came first.

The Familia in Yonkers and Mount Vernon set the meeting in an old, abandoned church basement off Warburton Avenue.

Brick walls, flickering fluorescent lights, folding chairs lined in uneven rows with the musty smell of water smothering the nostrils.

The Yonkers captains sat stiff when King entered.

No applause.

No greetings.

Just silence.

Vinnie stayed near the door.

Big Ty leaned against the wall, arms crossed, shadow swallowing half his face.

Gabi's tablet glowed softly, already recording everything.

King didn't sit.

"You all been eating off our supply," he said calmly. "Moving our product. Using our routes. Using our protection."

A man in the front row shifted.

"We built this before Miami"

King raised one finger.

The room froze.

"Before Miami," King repeated, nodding. "And now there is a Miami."

He stepped forward, boots echoing.

"You got two choices. You align. Or you get erased."

One man laughed nervously. That was the wrong move.

Vinnie moved first fast, silent, gun up, one shot into the floor inches from the man's foot.

The crack echoed like thunder.

King didn't flinch.

"I don't argue," he said. "I replace."

Silence swallowed the room.

A second man stood. "We're with you."

King nodded once. "Good. Then Mount Vernon falls in line too."

He turned to Big Ty. "Give the real they gold and clean the mess."

When King walked out, one body stayed behind.

No speeches.

No witnesses.

Just a new boss installed before sunrise.

Walking out of the church next stop is to Columbus.

Back on the jet King looks at the familia and says, "Columbus is not a negotiation."

It was a reminder.

Getting off the jet into a blacked-out bullet proof SUV booking it straight to the war room inside the GrindTime compound for the next meeting with the Columbus Familia Vinnie looked out the window laughing pointed to the playground off Shady Lane where they all first met reminiscing.

Pulling up to the command center they quickly get inside to the war room where the Columbus Familia waited.

King walked in stood at the head of the table instantly saying, "Anybody here forget who built this?" he asked.

Nobody answered.

Because they all remembered.

He pointed to a highlighted block.

"This crew's been skimming. Undermining prices. Talking to outsiders."

Dom swallowed. "They got family ties."

King stared through him.

"So did Rico."

The room went cold.

"Handle it and everybody come grab your Cuban," King said.

No theatrics. No yelling.

By morning, three lieutenants were gone.

Their replacements were already sworn in.

Columbus was locked in ready to proceed with expansion in the GrindTime Familia.

Next stop on the mission was Cleveland where things got intense.

Too many federal eyes.

Too many old enemies pretending to be neutral.

The meeting happened in a steel mill office overlooking dead machinery.

Jules laid out the numbers. “They’re leaking.”

King nodded. “Then we take care of loose ends.”

One lieutenant panicked. “This brings heat”

King stepped forward and grabbed him by the collar.

“You think heat scares me?” King whispered. “I was born in it.”

He released him.

Vinnie handled the rest.

Cleveland will be rebranded by the morning.

Moves had to be made hoping back in the jet the next stop was Detroit a vital piece on the chessboard.

Detroit was different.

Old muscle.

Old codes.

Men who didn't scare easy.

The meeting happened in an abandoned auto plant, rain leaking through the ceiling.

King walked the floor slowly as Vinnie and Big Ty scanned the room from both sides of King.

"You either stand with us, or we bury you under the weight of what we are building."

A leader stepped forward. "You think you're bigger than us?"

King smiled.

"No not at all fam," he said. "We are inevitable."

The fight didn't last long.

The Detroit O.Gs did not take too kind to King statement, but they respected his will, determination and the money they make with GrindTime.

Detroit niggas love making money and that was one thing GrindTime had plenty of.

Pulling out Gold Cuban Links and custom backwoods for the crews sealed Detroit.

Knocking out 4 cities already in 8 hours with two stops to be made in Atlanta, and Puerto Rico before morning sunrise sets the Familia was on a nonstop mission.

Atlanta was the next stop.

Hopping off the jet them Atlanta boys tried to play smart.

Too smart.

They showed up late.

Too many people.

Too much talking.

King, Vinnie and Big Ty let them talk and talk,

than they cut the lights.

When they came back on, two men were on their knees.

King's voice carried through the dark.

"This ain't a negotiation city anymore," he said. "It's a loyalty city."

One man begged.

King nodded at Ava.

She turned the tablet toward them showing him bank records, wire transfers, betrayal highlighted in red.

"You already chose," King said.

One shot.

The rest pledged allegiance immediately.

Atlanta was secured in under an hour.

Back at the jet King mentioned the last stop being the most important of the stops.

Puerto Rico was where our blood will be safe, and our people will have sovereignty. Puerto Rico was the piece to the puzzle that no one was ready for, that piece that would change the GrindTime Familia and anyone rocking with them life's forever.

Landing on the tarmac the island greeted the Familia with heat and gunmetal skies.

Puerto Rico wasn't just territory it was spiritual ground, supply chains, ports, future sovereignty.

The meeting took place at a coastal estate overlooking black water.

Cartel remnants. Political fixers. Church intermediaries.

All waiting.

King walked in with Mama GrindTime on FaceTime projected onto the wall.

That alone bent the room.

"You bring chaos," one man said carefully.

King smiled. "I bring order."

A translator repeated it in Spanish.

King stepped closer. "You move with us, you eat forever. You move against us your bloodline ends on this island."

One man reached for his glass.

Big Ty shot him before his hand got there.

No hesitation.

No warning.

King didn't even look at the body.

"Anybody else confused? he asked. Ports. Routes. Protection. We will be back to build on our businesses taking them to a whole different level soon please have a correct answer for us."

Back in the air, King sat alone thinking about the 6 cities they just hit in 24 hours.

Mama GrindTime's voice echoed in his mind:

Power ain't about expansion. It's about enforcement.

King stared out the window.

The cities were getting aligned.

The empire becoming unified.

These unknown hits are being figured out, everything will begin to work itself into a full circle.

"They coming," he said quietly.

Vinnie cracked his neck. "Good."

Big Ty smiled. "We ready."

" Never Play With Gods Creations."

Chapter Sixteen:

The Traitor in the Family

The Miami penthouse sat high above the chaos glass, marble, and silence. But this silence wasn't peace. It was the kind that screamed beneath the surface. The kind that crept in when betrayal slithered through bloodlines.

King GrindTime stood by the floor-to-ceiling windows, barefoot, robe open, the Atlantic wind pressing against the glass like a warning. His blunt burned slowly between his fingers, the ember glowing like the last pulse of someone who didn't see the knife coming.

He wasn't smoking to relax.

He was smoking to think.

To feel. To see.

Behind him, Jules entered with the kind of expression that didn't need words. King already felt it.

"Something's off," Jules muttered, setting a thick leather folder onto the marble table. The folder had weight not just physical, but spiritual.

Betrayal always did.

King turned slowly, eyes sharp, heavy with clarity. He extinguished the blunt in a lion-paw ashtray without breaking eye contact. "Show me."

Jules opened the folder like he was opening a casket. Line after line of offshore wire transfers. Crypto chains routed through obscure wallets.

Shell companies popping up like weeds briefly existing, then vanishing into digital smoke.

“Someone’s siphoning from the empire,”

Jules said, voice measured.

“It started small. Just a few thousand here, a few hundred there. But I cross-referenced the IP fingerprints. It’s all internal.”

Vinnie emerged from the hallway, dressed in black tactical gear, a matte pistol resting in his palm like an extension of his soul. His face was stone.

“That’s family,” he said, voice low. “That’s not some outsider. That’s somebody who’s eaten with us. Prayed with us. Laughed at our table.”

Big Ty leaned against the wall near the bar, his cigar glowing like a small sun. “Somebody close,” he added. “Real close. They moving’ like a ghost, but ghosts don’t get past me unless they know the codes.”

King sat down at the head of the obsidian dining table, fingers steepled beneath his chin. The weight of betrayal didn’t show on his face. Not yet. But the chill in his silence dropped the room’s temperature by degrees.

“How long?” he asked.

Jules replied, "Months. Maybe longer. I only found it because one of their transfers crossed through a flagged crypto node in Nigeria. They got sloppy."

King nodded slowly. "Sloppy means desperate. Desperate means scared. And scared means they know what happens when I find out."

He leaned back in the chair. "So, we don't let them know."

Big Ty raised an eyebrow. "Are you serious fam?"

"Dead serious," King said. "We let them keep skimming. Keep thinking they are safe. We follow every move, every message, every breath. We build the trap and then close it when they feel untouchable."

Vinnie smirked, spinning his blade in his fingers. "Old school. I like it. Let the mouse eat. Then snap the neck."

Jules slid another document across the table. "I traced the crypto wallets to three burner phones. All registered under fake names... but one of them pinged inside our distribution hub in Wynwood two weeks ago."

"Wynwood?" Big Ty sat up right now. "That's Ava's zone."

King's eyes narrowed slightly. "She been out of town. Jules, crosscheck all access logs for that building. Security, Wi-Fi pings, even trash pickup schedules. I want to know who was breathing in that space."

"Yes sir."

"Vinnie, pull all camera logs from every safe house, every warehouse, every lab for the last 90 days. Look for patterns. Look for ghosts."

"On it."

"Ty..." King stood slowly. His presence filled the room like a shadow came to life. "You start planting seeds in the minds of everyone. Whisper that we're auditing. Let the guilty sweat. Pressure brings mistakes."

Big Ty grinned. "That's how we smoke 'em out."

King walked back to the window, the ocean dark and endless in front of him. His voice was calm, almost too calm.

"They think blood means immunity. They think loyalty is a choice. But they forgot something."

He turned to face them. Cold fire in his eyes.

"I made this family. I bled for it. Built it from dirt, disappointment, and dead ends. If one of ours turned Judas... then Judas dies screaming."

Silence fell again. But this time, it had a pulse.

Outside, a thunderstorm began to gather over the ocean, its dark clouds rolling in like a curtain rising on Act Two of a tragedy.

Inside, King's empire was preparing for war not against rivals, but against the rot within.

Because the only thing more dangerous than an enemy? Was a traitor who knew your heart.

Chapter Seventeen:

The Los Reyes Meeting

South Beach, midnight.

The air carried that signature blend of ocean salt and street heat like perfume laced with gasoline. High-end imports crawled along Ocean Drive, purring like tigers on leashes. Neon signs buzzed above corner diners while sand-drenched waves whispered secrets to the shore. But on this night, the real power was shifting not under the stars but behind closed doors.

The matte-black Rolls-Royce Phantom purred to a halt in front of an unmarked building with obsidian glass and no visible signage. But King GrindTime didn't need a sign. He knew exactly where he was.

The Black Pearl Club.

There were no velvet ropes.

No Instagram stories. No influencers in line.

This place didn't exist to the public.

You couldn't buy your way in, you had to bleed your way in. Deals struck here reshaped entire cities, toppled governments, and birthed empires from whispers. And tonight, it was ground zero for a seismic shift in the underworld.

King stepped out of the Phantom, dressed in a tailored black silk shirt, unbuttoned just enough to reveal the GrindTime pendant hanging over his chest. His slacks were cut so sharp they could slice through steel. He adjusted the cuff of his Royal Oak Offshore, its face encrusted with crushed emeralds one of one.

Flanking him were his shadows:

Big Ty, broad as a warhorse, draped in a leather trench concealing the latest-gen armored vest. His face was stone, no emotion, no expression, just purpose.

Vinnie, dressed in street couture with an edge of madness. A silver blade flipped between his fingers like a habit, and a custom silenced pistol sat snug beneath his jacket. Vinnie didn't need orders he needed reasons not to start something.

As they entered the club, the world seemed to dim.

Inside, red velvet lighting bathed everything in blood. Dark walls bore murals of past kings, wars, and silent gods. A string quartet played softly in the background, but their faces were covered with black masks.

At the center of the room was the rooftop enclave, roped off by thick gold chains guarded by white-suited men with obsidian pistols. Sitting beneath a chandelier made from African elephant tusk and South American obsidian, was Alvaro Reyes the iron-fisted head of the Los Reyes Cartel.

His suit was ivory silk, hand-embroidered with golden threads forming Aztec glyphs across the sleeves. His smile didn't reach his eyes.

“King GrindTime,” Alvaro said, standing slowly with a raised hand.

“Miami’s ghost turned into the hurricane.”

King returned the gesture, grip firm and eyes locked. “Alvaro. You called this. So, talk.”

They sat. The table between them gleamed with untouched bottles of Clase Azul, chilled crystal glasses, and a small steel case emitting faint cold vapor.

The air felt like a prophecy.

Alvaro leaned in, eyes narrow. “You shook this city like a damn earthquake. Took Vasquez out like a rookie, swallowed his ports, redirected his crates. You moved in silence, and now Miami screams your name.”

King exhaled smoke from a slow burning backwood. “Legacy isn’t about who held the throne first. It’s about who dies holding it last.”

Alvaro’s fingers tapped the steel case slowly. “I have blood in this soil. Three generations of Reyes money buried in these docks, these streets, these courts.”

He poured himself a shot, still untouched by King.

“Your people are loyal. But loyalty is tested when power grows fast. You’re building fast, King. And fast growth can split empires like dry wood.”

King didn’t blink. “I build under pressure. Pressure makes diamonds. You came here with warnings what do you really want?”

Alvaro chuckled. “I want to see if the rumors are true.”

King raised an eyebrow. “Which ones?”

Alvaro’s smile faded.

“That you’re not just building an empire. You’re building a religion. I heard about your temples in Harlem. The underground one in Accra. I heard about your weed strains laced with scripture and blessing oil. Heard about your banks that only your people can touch. Are you trying to be a god, King?”

King leaned forward now, voice low and lethal. “Gods are created by desperate men. I didn’t ask for worship. I gave protection. I offered peace. But if they choose war”

He tapped the table.

“I baptize ‘em in fire.”

Alvaro’s jaw clenched. He reached into his pocket and unlocked his phone. The screen lit up. Three alerts.

Three shipments. Intercepted.

Each worth millions. Each hit strategically, without a trace.

He looked up slowly. King was already leaning back; arms spread across the booth like a throne.

“You thought I came here to negotiate. I came to confirm your seat... or replace it.”

Vinnie clicked his tongue, slow and steady.

Big Ty didn't move. But the tension in his jaw said he was ready for war.

Alvaro slammed his glass down. "You son of a"

King stood, calm as a sunrise. He flicked his blunt onto the marble floor where it hissed out like a serpent retreating.

"I don't do ultimatums, Alvaro. I give prophecies. And here it is you'll either partner with GrindTime Nation, or your bloodline becomes part of our soil."

Alvaro's eyes burned with rage. But behind that rage was fear.

King stepped closer and whispered in Alvaro's ear:

"Legacy ends when pride outweighs vision. Don't be Vasquez."

Then he turned and walked away.

Vinnie followed with a grin. Big Ty with silent thunder.

Behind them, Alvaro's guards scrambled. Orders were shouted. Phones were pulled. But it was already too late.

The city had chosen its new king.

And God help anyone who tries to reverse the crown.

" Grind louder than they gossip you will never lose."

Chapter Eighteen

Shadows Closing In

The Capitol building stood silent under a blanket of moonlight, but inside a private office deep within the west wing, chaos brewed in whispers.

Senator William Langston's fingers trembled over the smooth mahogany of his desk. The overhead light cast sharp shadows over the file open in front of him.

On its tab: **OPERATION: GRINDTIME – FEDERAL EYES ONLY.**

Inside? Photos. Charts. Audio transcripts. Satellite shots. Classified red flags.

He didn't need to open another page to feel the gravity. The storm that had erupted in Miami wasn't just another cartel war. It was evolution. Controlled chaos with a divine undertone.

"You're shaking, Senator."

Detective Elijah Carter's voice sliced through the room like a scalpel. Dressed in a sharp charcoal suit with no tie, his badge hidden, and a Glock strapped to his ankle, Carter wasn't just a federal liaison, he was a shadow soldier for the government's blackest programs.

Langston looked up, his voice thin. "You saw the Reyes files? The Black Pearl meeting?"

“I saw everything,” Carter replied, dropping a flash drive onto the table. “And I listened to Reyes’ last comm before going dark. He never even made it back to Colombia. Miami swallowed him.”

Langston’s jaw clenched. “King GrindTime didn’t just win that meeting. He declared divinity. Do you realize what that means?”

Carter’s cold eyes didn’t blink. “He made loyalty look like religion. That’s the difference. Gangsters build empires. Kings build faith.”

The senator stood and moved to the window. Beyond the bulletproof glass, the marble steps of the Capitol glowed white in the night. But all Langston could see was red. Red lines. Red maps. Red alerts. Everywhere King’s name surfaced, chaos followed. Not random, but methodical surgery.

Langston exhaled slowly. “We tried freezing his crypto accounts. He created his own coin backed by street currency and temple donations. We hit his shipping routes, and he bought the ports. We sanctioned his nonprofit arms, and they became registered sovereign ministries.”

Carter stepped closer. “Interpol, C.I.A, NATO, they all agree. We’re not fighting a man. We’re fighting a movement. And movements backed by scripture and bullets don’t die easily.”

Langston’s fingers tapped the file like a heartbeat. “So, what do we do?”

Carter's voice dropped an octave. "We go darker. No courtrooms. No press releases. Covert incursion only. We pull Project Ember light out of the vault. We go full-spectrum disruption: economic, spiritual, biological."

The senator froze. "Ember light was shut down after Geneva. You want to unfreeze a ghost program to hunt a living one?"

Carter didn't flinch. "GrindTime has outgrown law enforcement. We either become what he fears... or we pray his mercy includes us."

Langston stared into the night. "Then God help us all."

Meanwhile at the GrindTime Estate Miami

Steel gates hissed open as the final perimeter lockdown snapped into place. Miles from Washington, the GrindTime estate in Miami pulsed like a heart under armor every beat synchronized by power and paranoia.

Above ground, it looked like paradise. Palm trees swayed. Exotic weed scented the breeze. But underground?

Hell was getting organized.

The War Room, a circular, LED-lit bunker buried beneath the estate buzzed with encrypted data feeds, holographic intelligence, and the low hum of high-stakes chess.

At its center, King GrindTime stood like a general carved from shadow and will.

On the table floated a 3D map. Red dots marked global threats. Blue flickers indicated surveillance breaches. Gold glows pulsed where new temples rose.

"Replay the Reyes intercepts," King ordered.

Jules tapped the glass.

A replay unfolded: Reyes at the Black Pearl. His tone shifted from power to panic. His men were scrambling. The last words before silence:

"He's not a man. He's a plague with a purpose."

Then static.

Mama GrindTime entered through the back. Robe flowing. Hair wrapped in deep violet. Her eyes held the depth of ten lifetimes.

"They are watching' you like you the beast in Revelation," she said, voice deep and smooth. "But they forgot... beasts don't pray before they strike, and you do."

King turned to her. "I thought the Reyes meeting would slow 'em down."

Mama smirked. "You didn't slow 'em. You made 'em desperate."

Big Ty leaned forward, arms crossed over his chest. "That's when rats bite hardest. Desperate."

Vinnie, perched near the tech console, didn't even look up. "I say we shut the rats up. Permanently."

Jules cleared his throat. "You all need to see this."

The map zoomed in. Dots shifted. A new file opened: "Operation Ember light - Reactivated."

Mama GrindTime's eyes narrowed. "They unchained the devil."

"What is it?" asked Ty.

"Classified network protocol," Jules said. "Biological disruption. False-flag operations. Discredit and destroy tactics. No fingerprints. No recovery."

"They gon' try to crucify you," Mama GrindTime said.

King didn't blink. "Let 'em bring the nails. I'll flip the cross into a throne."

Silence thickened.

Then, King raised his hand.

All the red dots disappeared.

In their place, gold lights exploded across the map showed All of the Americas, Africa, India, Europe, Southeast Asia.

"We don't retaliate. We evolve," King said. "We don't shoot first. We build bigger. We plant so deep, even God has to ask us for directions."

Mama GrindTime chuckled low. "Say it again."

King's voice cut through the room.

"We don't play defense anymore.
We build faith that eats governments.
We turn loyalty into law.
And if they wanna bring war
We baptize it in fire."

The screen behind him updated again.

Los Angeles under siege.

Berlin surveillance compromised.

Tokyo GrindTime temple opening scheduled.

Puerto Rico locked and blessed.

Big Ty cracked his knuckles. "So, what's the move?"

King stepped back, eyes scanning his family.

"We disappear from their radar and then we reappear in every place they fear all at once."

A storm was coming.

But the GrindTime Empire?

They weren't running.

They were becoming the thunder.

Chapter Nineteen

The Empire's Evolution

"When the system tries to erase you,
Build your own system.
And make theirs obsolete."
— Mama GrindTime

GLOBAL TRANSMISSION – 6:00 AM EST

A sudden flicker danced across TV screens, smartphones, and news tickers worldwide. Regular programming halted. Logos glitched. The screen turned black.

Then, a symbol appeared: a burning crown wrapped in vines of gold, pulsing like a heartbeat. The crest of GrindTime.

"We interrupt your systems...
To introduce a new one."

King GrindTime stood center-screen, hooded, regal, fire behind his eyes. But this wasn't a threat. This was scripture.

"You've been ruled by the invisible hand.
Now meet the visible Kingdom.
No more banks without morals.
No more governments without mercy.
No more bloodshed without accountability.
This is the GrindTime Era."

The screen cut to footage: food being delivered to war-torn zones.

GrindTime medics setting up in favelas. Urban temples rising like phoenixes from ash. Children praying in newly built halls made of hempcrete and solar panels.

"We don't need to take over the world.
We just need to give it back to the people."

The broadcast lasted just 5 minutes.

But it was the most downloaded, replayed, encrypted, and feared broadcast since the moon landing.

VATICAN CITY – Noon

The Pope watched the transmission from a dim prayer room.

He didn't speak.

But he reached for a secure phone and called The Order which was a secret division of faith and finance long whispered about in Vatican corridors. One word left his lips:

"Contain."

JOHANNESBURG, SOUTH AFRICA – 7:02 PM Local Time

On a dusty hill just outside the city, a blacked-out convoy pulled up to an unfinished structure.

King stepped out first.

Behind him: Serenity, Mama GrindTime, Jules, Ava, and Dom.

Before him? A hundred village elders. Warriors. Generational leaders.

The temple they stood in front of.

GrindTime Africa the spiritual and economic gateway to the southern continent.

King handed over the gold-laced key not to security, not to politicians but to the women elders of the village.

“You don’t work for me,” he said. “I work for your legacy.”

Mama GrindTime poured libations on the dirt, then whispered into the ground, “Let our roots protect this soil.”

And the earth answered.

SAN JUAN, PUERTO RICO – Midnight

Dom GrindTime hosted an underground concert in the ruins of an old Spanish fort.

No stage. No ads. Just vibes.

But in the backroom? Financial papers were signed. Islands acquired. Shipping lanes secured.

The Caribbean, once split by colonizers, was being reconnected through family, not force.

LOS ANGELES – Sunset

Ava lit up Rodeo Drive not with shopping bags, but with purpose.

An entire strip had been rebranded overnight. GrindTime banners flew high. Influencers marched not for clout, but for community.

Her cologne “Loyalty” hit $5M in pre-orders. But she wasn’t chasing perfume money.

She was chasing influence.

“Every scent holds a story,” Ava said to the press. “And ours? Smells like revolution.”

GRINDTIME WAR ROOM – Miami

Back at HQ, Vinnie updated security protocols. Big Ty trained a new team of mercs baptized in both code and code-switching.

But Jules had the real news.

“They’re activating sleeper agents,” he said. “Interpol’s tracking our movement through biometric facial scans and blockchain forensics. But...”

He grinned.

“...our quantum ghost protocol’s ahead of them. Every time they blink, we evolve.”

King stood silent, staring at the map.

Then he turned to Serenity.

“Pull the youth into this. Give ‘em identity. Purpose. Legacy. Make ‘em remember they were royalty before they were ever born into struggle.”

Serenity nodded. "Already done. We are launching GrindTime Genesis schools next week, VR training, and mental health camps worldwide."

Mama GrindTime smiled. "You are building a future. Just don't forget the past."

King kissed her forehead.

"I am the past. I am the future. And I'll never let them erase either, today we as a family spread our reach, love and grind to the world sending a message to all get with us or sit your ass in the corner."

Secretly in Washington D.C.

There was an Emergency Briefing.

Langston stared at the screen in disbelief. "They've activated GrindTime Africa, Puerto Rico, LA, and there's word of a Vatican ally turning?"

Agent Carter growled. "He's not building an empire. He's creating a sovereign ecosystem. Churches, banks, armies, schools, every piece of the game."

Langston whispered, "What do we do now, these statements they just made trumps everything we just did?"

Carter slid a folder across the table.

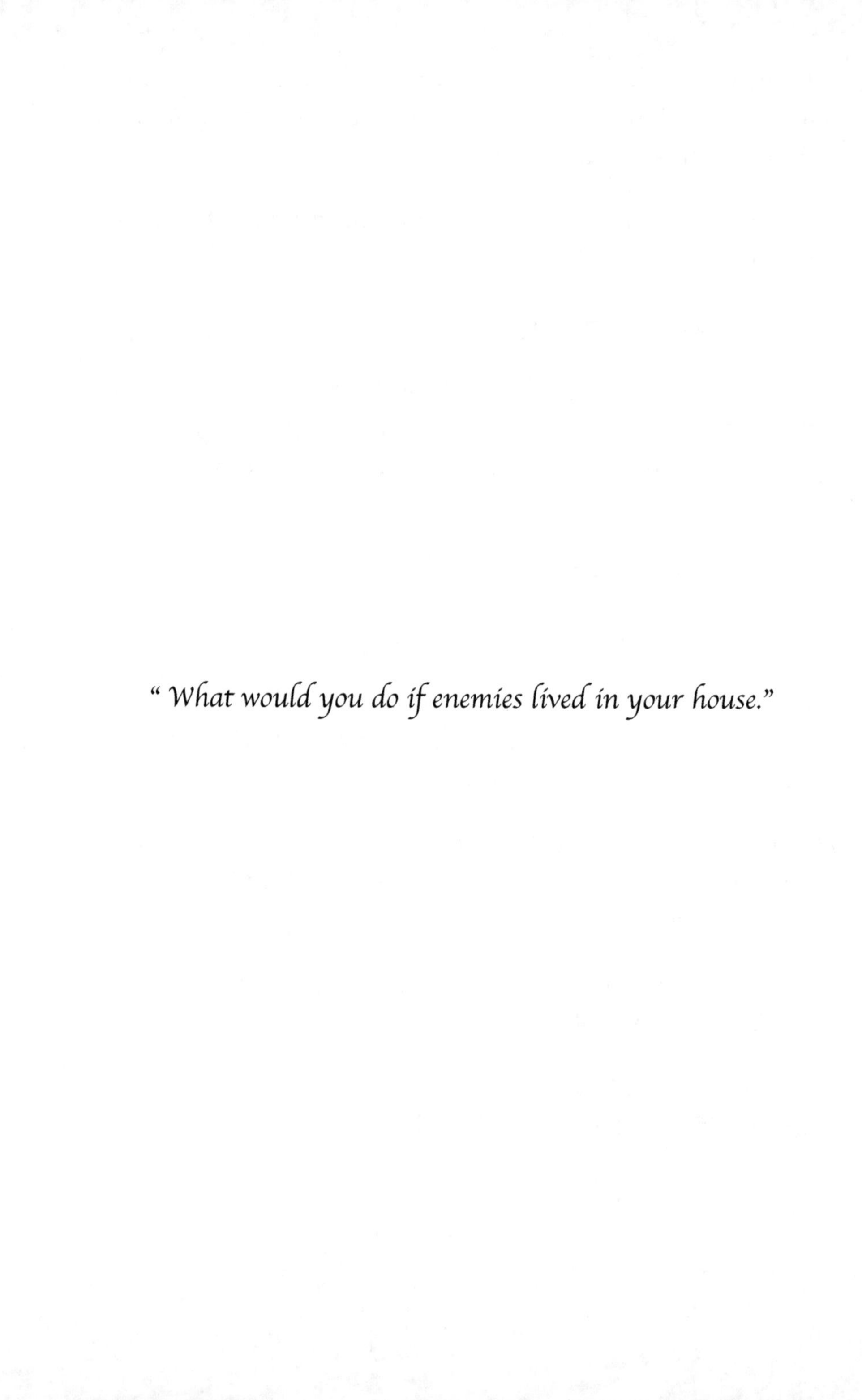

" What would you do if enemies lived in your house."

Chapter Twenty

The Betrayal Uncovered

The Miami skyline shimmered under the cloak of night, neon lights reflecting across the waves like the heartbeat of a city that never truly sleeps. Inside the top floor of the GrindTime penthouse, silence reigned not the peace of calm, but the pressure before a storm.

King GrindTime stood alone in the penthouse lounge, back turned to the door, staring out across Biscayne Bay. The ocean shimmered, endless and dark just like the thoughts flooding his mind. He wasn't wearing his usual chains tonight.

No gold.

No flash.

Just a black T-shirt, cracked knuckles, and a silence that threatened to rupture the air itself.

Behind him, the heavy double doors creaked open.

Jules entered, flanked by Dom and Ava. He held the black folder like it was radioactive.

"We confirmed it," Jules said. His voice was low, even. "Everything. The data trails. The dummy corporations. The routing codes. Offshore wallets. It all links back to... Eli."

King didn't flinch. He didn't even turn around.

"How much?" he asked.

"Seven point three million skimmed off the Tokyo deal," Jules replied. "Another twelve routed through fake PR grants. There's whispers he was lining up something in Lagos, too. He was building a shadow empire under the family's name."

Still, King said nothing.

Dom stepped forward, anger simmering. "We could've lost half our ports. What if Reyes' enemies got that intel? What if NATO did?"

Ava clenched her fists. "He gave 'em our codes, King. That's not ambition. That's treason."

King finally spoke.

"Where is he?"

Jules looked down. "He just arrived. He thinks he's here to debrief on the Berlin launch."

King exhaled sharply through his nose. "Good. Bring him in."

Fifteen minutes later in the GrindTime Interrogation Room in the lower level, the room was carved out of obsidian-black concrete, soundproofed, lit by a single hanging bulb. A glass of water sat untouched on a steel table in front of Eli GrindTime, who leaned back like a man unaware of his own eulogy.

He wore a velvet tracksuit, white and gold, with his initials stitched into the sleeve, E.G.T. Confidence in every movement. A fake smile on his lips.

When King entered, the air shifted. The silence got sharper. Colder.

“Cuzzo,” Eli said, flashing that grin. “Been a minute. Heard we're locking in Berlin, huh?”

King didn’t respond. He just walked to the table and set the folder down.

Then he opened it.

And turned it toward Eli.

Eli’s smirk faltered as his eyes scanned the document's screenshots of wire transfers, IP logs, signatures traced to encrypted burners, even photos of a midnight meeting in Santo Domingo with one of Reyes’ rivals.

“You know what this is?” King asked, voice level.

Eli’s lips parted, searching for words. “Look, bro it’s not what it looks like—”

King slammed a palm down so hard the steel table rang like a bell. “Don’t insult me.”

Eli flinched.

“I took you in when you had nothing’,” King continued. “You were a broke tagalong in Yonkers wearing’ knockoff Timbs and beggin’ to be put on. Mama fed you like her own. I taught you the grind. Let you eat at my table. And you tried to poison the plate.”

“I didn’t” Eli choked. “I wasn’t giving it to enemies, I just... I wanted my own! Something that was mine. You don’t know what it’s like, always being in your shadow.”

King leaned in.

“You think this shadow was free?”

A long silence.

“You think I didn’t bleed for this empire? Lose sleep, bodies, blood and years? I gave you a kingdom and you tried to sell the bricks. That ain’t hunger. That's a weakness.”

Eli looked down. His voice cracked. “I didn’t want to hurt you...”

“Then why do I feel stabbed in the back?”

Flashback: The Bond That Was

King and Eli, age 16, riding bikes through the streets of Columbus. Ducking gunshots, skipping meals, and swearing they’d rise together.

“We blood, forever,” Eli had said, fist to chest.

“Then act like it,” King had said, fist bumping his cousin beneath a streetlight.

Back in the room, King stood.

Vinnie and Big Ty entered like ghosts. No words needed.

Eli’s eyes widened. “Please, King. Exile me. Send me to the jungle. I’ll vanish. I swear. Please. Please.”

King didn't blink. "You'll vanish, alright."

Big Ty dropped the duffel bag on the floor. He Opened it. Pulled out the .45 King used in his first ever deal engraved with the GrindTime logo.

He handed it to King.

King took it slowly. Walked to Eli.

Eli sobbed now. "Please, I'm your cousin"

King raised the gun.

"You were," he said.

POP.

Blood painted the back wall like a Jean-Michael Basquiat original.

Eli slumped.

Big Ty wiped the gun down. Vinnie lit a blunt.

Silence.

"Take him to the Everglades," King muttered. "Feed the swamp."

Back Upstairs on the Penthouse Balcony

King stood outside, shirt off, body still covered in a thin sheen of sweat. The city stretched beneath him.

Alive. Loud. Restless.

Mama GrindTime appeared behind him.

“Handled?”

King nodded once.

“He was family.”

“He was a threat.”

She rested a hand on his shoulder. “You did what you had to.”

He didn’t respond.

He just stared into the horizon.

“In this life,” he whispered, “loyalty ain’t just a word. It’s breath. You betray it... you don’t deserve to breathe.”

Behind him, the estate came alive again. Plans. Calls. Strategy. Expansion.

But something had changed.

The empire wasn’t just built on hustle anymore.

Now, it was built on vengeance.

And the streets were about to learn

Loyalty is thicker than blood.

And blood always stains.

Chapter Twenty-One

Puerto Rico Takeover

"Every island got roots... we just came to water 'em with pressure."

The jet sliced through the Puerto Rican sky like a blade wrapped in silk. Beneath it, San Juan glittered beneath the late afternoon sun blue waves crashing with rhythm, palm trees swaying like whispers from their ancestors.

Inside the Gulfstream G650, silence reigned. But it wasn't tension.

It was calculation.

King GrindTime sat in the leather recliner, eyes half-closed, blunt burning slow between his fingers. Beside him sat Big Ty, arms crossed over his chest like a war-ready titan, and Jules, tapping away at a custom tablet with satellite links, encrypted ledgers, and the Church's global financial models. The cabin smelled like luxury, cologne, pressure, and a quiet sense of vengeance still fresh from Eli's betrayal.

No one spoke.

The death of Eli hadn't slowed the mission, it sharpened it.

This trip wasn't about retaliation.

It was about ascension.

As the jet touched down, blacked-out SUVs were already lined up on the private runway. At the front stood Santiago Rivera the silent storm of Puerto Rico's underworld. A man who wore wealth like a second skin and power like a whisper.

"Mi Hermano," Santiago greeted in a thick, controlled accent, embracing King. Gold rings glinted on every finger, but his eyes were calculating, already reading the energy.

"They told me you conquered Miami," Santiago said with a careful smirk.

King didn't miss a beat. "I didn't conquer it. I reminded them who it belonged to."

Santiago laughed, but tension sat beneath his smile. He knew King wasn't here for handshakes and island hospitality. He was here to rewrite legacies.

Inside Santiago's clifftop villa, everything smelled like old money and older secrets. The ocean slammed against the rocks below like a war drum. Walls of glass gave way to panoramic views of a kingdom ready for harvest.

King sat back on a white leather couch while Big Ty posted up near the glass like a sentinel and Jules laid out folders on the marble table with documents of offshore crypto banks, medical cultivation licenses, private security contracts, and diplomatic loopholes through the Church.

Santiago poured three glasses of Reserva de la Familia rum, aged longer than most alliances. "So," he said, sliding a glass across to King, "why Puerto Rico? Why now?"

King lit a new blunt. The fire reflected in his shades. "Because it's time."

"Time for what?" Santiago asked.

King exhaled. "Legacy. We ain't just building a weed empire. We are building sovereignty. Religion. Rebirth. Puerto Rico ain't just an island it's the future headquarters of the Green Empire."

Santiago's brow lifted. "You're talking war with the old guard."

"I'm talking about replacing it."

King leaned forward.

"Puerto Rico's got more than just ports and pretty beaches. It's got farmland, labs, airspace, shipping lanes. It's a bridge between the East and West. And it's still controlled by ghosts from a system that was never built for us. But I've got a new system built on truth, protection, and profit. Backed by God and sealed in blood."

Santiago reached for the folders. Page after page laid out King's plan: medical dispensaries under religious protection, air travel through private charter loopholes, Church based offshore trust networks, community funded grow hubs camouflaged as eco-resorts, and a militia of believers trained in law, combat, and agriculture.

And stamped on every plan GrindTime insignia, gilded in green.

Santiago finally looked up. "And what if I say no?"

King didn't blink. "Then I'll own it anyway."

He took another drag, voice low but laced in certainty.

"I don't need permission. I offered you a legacy."

Silence.

Santiago walked over to a bookshelf, pulled a hidden switch, and revealed a wall safe. Inside, he grabbed a small black box and opened it inside was a golden family ring, encrusted with emeralds.

"My grandfather wore this when he took the island from the Spaniards... before the cartels turned it into a trade zone. If I give this to you, it means you're the new patron."

King stood.

"I don't need symbols. I need faith. And land."

Santiago nodded slowly, eyes locked. "Then you got both."

That night, King stood barefoot on the balcony, shirt unbuttoned, wind licking at his chains. Below, the sea roared like prophecy. Behind him, the deal was sealed.

Jules had already secured the land titles through shell companies and trust law via the Church. Big Ty had armed local security in every town bordering cartel pockets. And Santiago?

He was now the island's new spiritual viceroy under the GrindTime umbrella.

King's phone buzzed.

Mama GrindTime.

“You handle your business?” she asked.

King’s voice was calm, steady. “Handled.”

“You didn’t come for war this time, did you?” she asked, already knowing the answer.

King exhaled slowly. “No. I came for dominion.”

Mama’s voice softened. “Then remember... dominion demands discipline. Don’t let your own roots choke you.”

“I won’t.”

“And don’t forget,” she added, “you’re still being watched. By them. By the ones who lost the last war. The ones who didn’t die.”

King’s jaw tensed.

“I know. That’s why I brought the Church with me.”

She chuckled. “Then build in silence... until your light blinds the world.”

He ended the call.

Then whispered:

“Puerto Rico ain’t just ours now... it’s sacred land. Green Empire land. And from this soil, a new world is gon’ rise.”

The moonlight lit his face as thunder rolled in the distance.

And somewhere far away deep in the shadows of governments, cartels, and fallen kings an alarm went off. King GrindTime had just claimed another chessboard. And the world was running out of moves.

Chapter Twenty-Two

The Los Angeles Play

City of dreams.

Land of lies.

Home of the easily bought and the secretly broken.

Los Angeles didn't move like the other cities. It shimmered. It performed. It pretended. But beneath its polished veneers and Botox smiles, it was rotten with desperation. Here, power didn't wear bulletproof vests, it wore red carpet tuxedos and billion-dollar smiles.

King GrindTime didn't land in L.A. with an army.

He landed with a prophecy.

Fresh off the Puerto Rico conquest where sacred soil was claimed and a global empire rooted in sovereignty had begun to rise, word had spread.

The Los Reyes Council, that elite summit of global cartel bosses and power brokers, had heard the whispers. Puerto Rico had flipped green. Santiago Rivera had joined the Church. The Church now had ports, labs, and ocean routes.

The old heads wanted in.

And L.A.?

L.A. was next on the board.

The GrindTime jet touched down at Van Nuys Airport just after midnight. The sky was bruised with smog and secrets.

City lights flickered like false promises. As the doors opened, a wave of warm Pacific air wrapped around them soft, scented, synthetic.

King stepped off the plane in silence. Black-on-black designer fit. Fresh Royal Runtz rolled tight between his fingers.

Behind him came Ava GrindTime, his daughter and the new queen of perception warfare. She didn't just influence culture; she owned the damn mirror it looked into.

Dressed in obsidian silk and savage ambition, Ava scrolled through three phones while booking meetings that would shape Hollywood's next five years.

Big Ty followed, draped in casual intimidation bearded, broad, and built like he body-slammed secrets for fun.

Vinnie adjusted his chain and shades, already peeping out the skyline like it owed him rent. "City fake as hell," he muttered. "But that bag is real."

They slid into a bulletproof Escalade and moved through the city like shadows. Paparazzi flashes bounced off tinted glass. Billboards glowed with empty faces and fake smiles.

Sitting across from King, Ava never looked up from her screen. "This city's all glitter and gaslighting," she said. "But behind the scenes? That's where the real kings eat."

King took a slow pull from his blunt, smoke curling like prophecy. "Which means it's ripe."

The Citadel they pulled up to was a fortress in disguise; an exclusive rooftop lounge nestled above Beverly Hills. No press. No outsiders. Just insiders who made empires move with a nod or a whisper.

Tonight, Ava had arranged a curated guest list:

- A Netflix VP known for laundering agendas through programming
- Two major label execs who owed Ava quiet favors
- The mayor's chief of staff, hungry for exposure and hush money
- A private equity firm owner whose offshore accounts already moved through GrindTime'
- New Puerto Rican shell networks

When the GrindTime Familia stepped into the room, the music didn't stop.

But the energy shifted.

No, they were not famous.

They didn't have to be. Power recognizes power.

Ava introduced King not like a guest, but like a godfather. “This is my father. The real architect. The reason you’ve heard of me.”

One exec tried to joke. “I thought you were the muscle behind the media...”

King said nothing. Just stared until the chuckle dried up like spit on concrete.

Big Ty positioned himself by the entrance. Vinnie took mental snapshots of everyone in the room, from wristwatches to body language.

Ava smiled, that signature smirk of someone who owned outcomes.

“L.A. is illusions,” she said. “And tonight, we’re building new ones.”

Within two hours:

- GrindTime Media acquired partial ownership in two music agencies

- A director pledged three film packages to Ava’s vision scripts already ghostwritten by her

- GrindTime Church was offered tax-exempt land for a “Wellness & Healing Center” in Malibu

- A new cannabis licensing loophole was opened via the mayor’s staff to push the Green Empire’s royal strains throughout California

And in the center of it all?

King GrindTime, calmly orchestrating every handshake like a silent symphony.

He didn't speak often.

But when he did?

Deals inked themselves.

Later that night, King stood at the edge of The Citadel's rooftop. The skyline blinked beneath him like a dying star.

Below, producers popped bottles.

Models pretended to laugh.

Agents whispered into phones they thought weren't being tapped.

Ava joined him, sipping a rose-colored cocktail. The air smelled like pine, citrus, and influence.

"We could own this city in thirty days," she said.

King looked at her. "You already do."

She smiled, but something flickered in her eyes. "I got a message from one of the Los Reyes council members. The Santiago moves in Puerto Rico... it scared them. But it also woke them up. They wanna come to L.A. next they said they want in."

King's eyes narrowed. "Did they say how they'd show loyalty?"

Ava handed him her phone. On screen: a wire receipt eight figures sent to the GrindTime Church.

“No words,” she said. “Just the transfer and a name.”

King looked at the name.

A Mexican logistics giant.

Disguised as a faith-based nonprofit.

Ready to move anything from anywhere.

“Good,” he said. “Then it’s time we light the West up green.”

Vinnie stepped onto the balcony. “What’s next?”

King looked out at the city, as if he could already see GrindTime flags waving above Capitol Records, The Grove, and Compton projects.

“We’re building the illusion first,” he said. “Then we own the reality.”

Big Ty cracked his knuckles. “Vegas still on deck?”

King nodded. “Vegas, then back East. But L.A.? This ain’t just a flex.”

He turned, eyes cold.

“This is the beginning of the media war. We conquer how they think. Then they never fight back again.”

As the SUVs pulled out into the sleepy morning streets, the Strip Clubs of Sunset still bumped after-hours playlists.

Drunks staggered home with dreams of stardom. A billboard unveiled a new Ava GrindTime production.

The city didn't know yet.

But it had already been bought.

By nightfall, GrindTime would have its grip on California's influence pipeline music, fashion, weed, wellness, politics, and social media.

And across the world?

The Reyes Council watched in silence.

Because Puerto Rico had bowed.

And now?

Los Angeles had been baptized.

Next stop?

Vegas.

Where the dice never stop rolling... and the house always belongs to the King.

“ Those who walk with purpose fear no man.”

Chapter Twenty-Three

The Vegas Gambit

"Power ain't just played at the tables it's won in blood and silence."

The Las Vegas air cracked with a dry electricity as the GrindTime jet descended onto McCarran's private runway.

Neon lights bled across the desert horizon, and the Strip pulsed like a golden artery of greed and lust but tonight, a darker power touched down. One that didn't blink. One that didn't ask permission.

King GrindTime stepped off the jet in a charcoal-black suit stitched with midnight threading. A new Rolex glinted on his wrist, but it was the calm in his walk that made the ground tremble. Big Ty followed, chewing on a cigar fat enough to be a weapon, vest tight under his hoodie. Vinnie brought up the rear, gloved hands cradling a silver briefcase, his other hand never far from his waistline. This wasn't tourism.

This was a goddamn coup.

A matte-black Rolls-Royce Phantom waited at the runway edge. The driver didn't speak. Just opened the door and dipped his head.

Inside the vehicle, King lit a slow burning backwood filled with Green Empire OG and looked out the tinted window.

Vegas shimmered like a lie told beautifully. But lies were meant to be broken.

They weren't going to DeLuca first.

They were headed to the "The Vault," first a high-stakes speakeasy buried under an abandoned art gallery off Sahara Avenue. There, a man named Tino Barranza waited the Cuban Mexican plug who ran Vegas' street-side narco trade, gun imports, and debt collection rings. He wasn't old money like DeLuca. He was new violence.

Tino ran things out of a room flooded in red light, surrounded by murals of saints and skeletons. Three men sat behind him. All armed. All sweating.

"You showed up late," Tino said in a thick accent, swirling rum in a lowball glass. "That usually means disrespect."

King didn't sit. "Or power. We had other cities to bury."

Tino chuckled, but it didn't touch his eyes. "I heard what happened in Puerto Rico. The Los Reyes meeting was just four days ago. You shook the world. Even got South American bosses whispering your name. You think that buys you Vegas?"

King stepped forward. "I don't think. I already bought it. I'm just waiting on receipts."

The room shifted. Tino's men reached toward their belts, but Vinnie was faster.

Bang. Bang. Bang.

Three headshots. Clean. No hesitation. No words.

Tino dropped behind the desk as chaos erupted.

Big Ty flipped the table and opened fire with his Glock-19, lighting the red-lit room with flash after flash. King moved like a shadow low, silent, decisive. Two more guards stormed in from the hallway and caught Vinnie's wrath before they could yell.

Smoke. Blood. Silence.

Tino crawled out, hands up, screaming, "Okay! Okay! You win!"

King stood over him, muzzle to his forehead.

"I don't play dice with rats," King said coldly. "Vegas ain't yours anymore."

Big Ty dropped a GrindTime Church medallion onto Tino's chest. "Tell the next fool who tries to run shit confess before you get condemned."

They left the bodies cooling behind them and drove to the Bellagio. Not to hide. To finish.

At the top of the hotel, Vincent DeLuca was waiting in his Romanesque penthouse suite, sipping 100-year-old Scotch in a robe made of real cashmere and old secrets. He was the face of Vegas' upper echelon part mafia, part monarch, part myth.

"You make a hell of an entrance," DeLuca said as King stepped into the suite, blood still drying on his collar.

"I make history," King replied.

DeLuca motioned to the leather seats. “Word travels fast. Heard you baptized the underground tonight.”

“I don’t come to ask,” King said, dropping a dossier onto the table. “I come to restructure.”

Inside the folder:

- Offshore laundering routes routed through DeLuca’s casino shells,
- Church-based wellness clubs camouflaged as strip lounges,
- GrindTime flower strains ready for exclusive Vegas licensing,
- And signed allegiance offers from Puerto Rico, Miami, and L.A.

DeLuca studied the papers like scripture. “You’re trying to build a holy empire out of sin.”

“I already did, and if I recall this is exactly what they did to us. Wrapped all these I.Ds, codes, laws, stories, holidays and bullshit into one fat ass present” King said. “You either help sanctify it... or get swept away.”

There was a pause then DeLuca smirked.

“Seventy-thirty?”

King nodded. “We own the halls. You keep your name on the doors.”

DeLuca stood and shook King's hand with a subtle bow. "Welcome to Vegas, Your Highness."

That week, the Strip was quietly baptized in GrindTime glory:

- Casino vaults rerouted to offshore Clean Hands accounts.
- Escort networks were rebranded as "Healing Ambassadors" of the Church.
- Nightclubs began hosting Church-approved "baptisms" with bottle service.
- And politicians? Bought in silence.

On the balcony of the Waldorf suite, Big Ty smoked over the skyline. "Damn... the city doesn't even know it just got sold."

King stepped beside him. "They'll learn."

From the shadows of Brickell to the beaches of Puerto Rico to the sin-soaked skyline of Vegas, a message was clear:

This wasn't just a takeover.

It was a prophecy unfolding.

And the Church of the GrindTime Empire?

Had just claimed the desert.

“ FAMILY.”

Chapter Twenty-Four:

The Rise of a Nation

"When loyalty becomes law, borders don't matter. Nations rise from belief."

The sun climbed over Puerto Rico like it was bowing to a higher authority. And in truth? It was.

On a cliffside in Rincón, where waves roared against stone and mist danced with the wind, King GrindTime stood barefoot in a white robe. The soft rustle of palm leaves moved in sync with the rhythm of ocean tides. In one hand, he held a steaming mug of dark Puerto Rican tea. In the other, a thick blunt of Royal Blood OG, rolled to perfection.

He didn't speak. He didn't need to. Because below him? A movement was growing.

The estate behind him buzzed with life. Armed guards in tactical gear scanned the perimeter. Trucks offloaded crates of lab-tested pharmaceuticals, designer strains, and encrypted server towers marked with Church symbols. Inside, war rooms pulsed with global intel. Surveillance feeds from five continents rotated across digital walls.

This wasn't just a base.

It was the capital of a new order.

Jules stepped onto the terrace, his suit wrinkled, eyes sunken, tablet clutched in hand. A new scar marked his neck souvenir from a close call in Panama.

"We got static in Vegas," he said, scrolling with a grimace. "D.E.A snatched one of our brokers. But Gabi already got the judge under review. We'll walk him in 24."

King exhaled smoke slowly, his eyes locked on the horizon.

"And D.C.?"

"Senator Langston's folding," Jules replied. "His aides are leaking. His foundation just accepted a donation from one of our shell trusts."

King cracked a smile. "Let the heat boil a little longer. Fear is how you teach obedience."

Just then, Big Ty strolled out, gold chains bouncing, pastelillo in one hand, Glock tucked under the other.

"Damn, Jules. You look like your soul been stressin' more than your body."

Jules grunted, "I ain't slept since Berlin."

Big Ty took a bite, mouth full. "That's cause we ain't runnin' a crew anymore."

He pointed out at the ocean, where a GrindTime freighter ship glided into port, its side painted with a crown wrapped in vines of smoke.

"We are buildin' a fucking nation."

King turned, eyes razor sharp. "Exactly."

Inside the main war room, Gabi GrindTime stood at the head of the black marble table, her presence precise, her aura colder than steel. Behind her: multiple legal teams, political advisors, and cyber teams monitored global chatter.

“Puerto Rico is locked in,” she reported. “We’ve built more infrastructure in 90 days than their government did in 20 years. The people are ours. Not through fear. Through loyalty.”

“And the world?” King asked.

“Interpol’s hesitating. MI6 is cautious. But it’s the Church Diplomatic Immunity strategy that’s freezing everyone,” she said, eyes focused. “Under international ecclesiastical protections, GrindTime leaders now qualify as spiritual diplomats.”

King nodded. “Good. Then let’s make it law.”

They moved swiftly.

By sundown, the GrindTime Church Charter was recognized by offshore nations as a faith-based humanitarian and medical organization. With 508(c)(1)(A) protections and U.N. advisors under payroll, GrindTime Ambassadors now crossed borders without search or seizure. Every smuggled crate was labeled “church medical outreach.” Every safe house now a sanctuary. Every armed convoy? A protected pilgrimage. Much like the systems put in place today but better and for the people.

But global power never goes unchecked.

In Geneva, cartel bosses huddled in candlelit tunnels beneath a luxury vineyard. Colombian dons, Russian black-market moguls, the Yakuza, and Balkan war profiteers all sat under one ceiling.

“GrindTime has gone too far,” whispered Dmitri Sokolov, the Russian chem kingpin.

“They’ve taken Vegas, flipped Panama, buried our networks in San Juan,” said El Búho, an aging but sharp-eyed cartel legend.

“Their Church is a shield,” a French trafficker growled. “Their Nation Project is not just profitable, it's... righteous. And that makes it dangerous.”

Across the room, a black envelope arrived. No name. No stamp. Just a GrindTime wax seal.

Inside: A map of the globe.

Marked in gold: Every GrindTime-controlled zone.

Marked in red: Every zone the cartel once ruled... now lost.

At the bottom?

One line handwritten by King:

“Convert... or be cleansed.”

Back in Puerto Rico, Dom GrindTime entered the war room with a cocky grin. “L.A. and Vegas are secured. Ava just launched Royal Blood Lifestyle at the Berlin Gala. The whole damn entertainment worlds on our prayer list now.”

"And the streets?" King asked, still calm.

"We feed both sides," Dom grinned. "Dispensaries for peace. Pressure for betrayal. Nobody loyal goes hungry. We even got ex-cartel soldiers joining our security squads. You flipped 'em with jobs, Pop."

King nodded.

"And education?"

"GrindTime Academies open in ten cities next week," Jules added. "STEM, coding, trade skills, mental health, all free. Kids wear robes with the Crown on their chest."

By the end of that quarter, the world saw the rollout of The Nation Project:

- GrindTime IDs – Faith-backed spiritual passports offering travel protection.
- GrindTime Exchange – A crypto/commodity hybrid system backed by cannabis, gold, and water.
- GrindTime Labs – Medical centers testing weed based treatments for trauma, cancer, and anxiety.
- GrindTime Studios – Media powerhouses building faith, fire, and influence.

Wherever the family touched ground, they didn't just profit.

They converted.

Mama GrindTime called from Columbus, her voice a soothing storm through satellite lines.

"You are settin' roots in places they ain't never thinkin' you'd even visit," she said. "Just remember, baby... roots grow deep. But when they rise? They break concrete."

King stood on the balcony of his Puerto Rican fortress, watching a new GrindTime Medical Center being built by former gang members and local families, all wearing the same crest.

"I don't want concrete," he whispered.

"I want the world to grow."

Mama paused. "Then get ready for the world to bleed."

Meanwhile...

- Vinnie was in Marseille, France securing underwater shipping routes and flipping former pirates into protectors.

- Big Ty moved through Panama, establishing pressure depots in old military zones and hosting warlords in peace dinners under Church banners.

- Ava GrindTime shook the European elite, converting fashion houses and film studios into grind-based power centers.

- Serenity GrindTime began training in Bogotá alongside a team of youth ambassadors reading children's mental health books from the Minds That Shine series to packed crowds of students, educators, and media. When she smiled, politicians leaned in. When she spoke, journalists wrote headlines. The daughter of King GrindTime wasn't just being raised; she was already leading nations.

- And King himself sat with African tribal kings, South American governors, and Caribbean revolutionaries offering something no one else had.

Sovereignty.

Purpose.

A future.

As the sun dipped over the Puerto Rican horizon, fireworks burst across the sky. Streets filled with music and flags marked with the gold and green of GrindTime. Families danced. Grandmothers prayed. Children wore robes.

A radio echoed through the village speakers:

> "The Nation of GrindTime has risen. Long live the Family."

King watched from the rooftop. He lit a fresh blunt. Took one deep pull.

And whispered:

"Now we global."

" If power cost you everything, would you still chase it?"

Chapter Twenty-Five

War Crowned in Blood

The sky over Columbus, Ohio, was gray.

Not from rain.

Not from clouds.

But from the thick smoke of a thousand unanswered sins. Sirens wailed in the distance, news drones circled the skyline like vultures, and below, every corner, every alley, every rooftop whispered one name in terrified awe "GrindTime."

But this wasn't just a funeral. This was a declaration.

72 Hours Earlier in Beirut, Lebanon

The GrindTime banner now flew above clubs in Berlin, clinics in Brazil, and research labs in Nairobi. But the blood started boiling in Beirut.

King sat in a luxury suite atop the Intercontinental Hotel, deep in negotiation with an arms dealer named Ziya Hassan, former MI6 asset, now freelancing for cartel and government alike.

Across the room, Jules monitored satellite footage, Ava typed into a secure network, and Gabi whispered with UN contacts to delay an arms embargo vote.

Then everything shattered.

A sniper round tore through the window glass and exploded, slicing Ava's cheek. Chaos. Vinnie tackled King to the floor, screaming, "DOWN!"

Three more shots followed each one closer, more precise.

But the shooter had misjudged.

King didn't panic. He moved like war was a rhythm only he could hear.

"Phase Black," he growled.

Jules hit a button on his tablet.

Within seconds, five hotel floors shut down. Doors sealed. Power cut. Cameras scrambled. An entire GrindTime mercenary unit stormed in, guided by Serenity's voice through encrypted comms.

"Targets on rooftop 19. Wind northbound. He's solo. Masked."

Serenity, only fourteen, had built the software that tracked heat signatures better than DARPA.

King's soldiers breached the stairwell. Flashbangs. Gunfire.

The assassin was ex-Special Forces, tattooed with CIA sigils and cartel ink. When cornered, he detonated a pulse bomb, wiping nearby electronics. But not before Gabi hacked his transmitter tracing it back to three sources: the U.S. Department of Energy, a cartel cell in Tijuana, and a private military contractor in Virginia with ties to the President.

24 Hours Later back in D.C.

They didn't wait.

The country was still processing the Beirut attack news anchors stammering through "unconfirmed" reports, intelligence agencies pointing fingers, but behind closed doors, silence echoed louder than any denial.

Meanwhile, King was already in the belly of the beast.

He walked through the security gates of the White House Donor Gala not as a man of war, but as a sovereign spiritual dignitary.

Ambassador GrindTime, recognized by six nations and two microstates.

His ID badge glimmered with gold trim, embossed with the sacred seal of the GrindTime Church: a roaring lion above a crown of thorns.

He wore all black tailored, satin-threaded, silent. No chain.

No diamonds.

Just power in motion.

Around him, America's elite mingled, sipping aged scotch and whispering under chandeliers paid for by lobbyist checks and oil money.

Hedge fund titans. Senators. Secretaries. High-ranking generals.

A former Vice President in retirement.

And yet every single one stepped aside as he passed.

The ballroom was lined with white marble and gold fixtures. Music played a subtle string quartet rendition of "Ave Maria." But King didn't hear it. He walked straight toward the back.

Senator William Langston, face pale and sweaty, waited in a corner booth. His drink untouched. His hands clenched together in a prayer he no longer believed in.

Behind King, Big Ty stood with his eyes locked on every exit and earpiece in the room. Vinnie, clean-shaven in a priest collar, sipped a flute of champagne while sliding microchips into key dignitaries' jackets silent surveillance cloaked as etiquette.

King sat down across from Langston.

"I thought you said we'd finalize next week," Langston muttered, voice cracking.

King didn't even blink. "I didn't come to finalize. I came to baptize."

Langston looked confused until King opened a black case.

Inside: an executive order.

A Federal Religious Sovereignty Accord. Signed by three interim cabinet members. It granted GrindTime's Church total immunity, legal, financial, and diplomatic.

Langston shook his head. "This... bypasses the Senate."

King leaned forward. "That's the point."

A pause.

Then he slid Langston a thumb drive.

“What’s this?”

“Insurance,” King said flatly. “Thirty-eight terabytes of every dirty operation your colleagues ever funded in Guatemala, Ukraine, and Cleveland signed, stamped, time coded.”

Langston’s hands trembled.

“You leak this and the whole country burns,” he whispered.

King stood.

“That’s not a threat, Senator. That’s a prophecy.”

The string quartet shifted music without cue.

Now it was a soft instrumental of “God Save the King.”

As King walked away, several international envoys turned to greet him bowing their heads, extending hands.

An Italian arms magnate whispered, “You’ve done what no black man has ever done in this city.”

King didn’t look back.

He whispered only once:

“This city just got baptized in royal blood.”

Now back in Columbus, Ohio

Twenty-four hours later, smoke from a thousand candles lit up the Columbus skyline. Church bells were silenced not by city officials, but by decree. Every barbershop, corner store, and gas station within twenty blocks was shut down. Black SUVs with foreign plates lined the streets. Drones hummed overhead. Rooftop snipers watched with scopes bearing sacred sigils.

Because today?

They were burying Eli.

And the GrindTime family had returned home.

The funeral was held in a once-abandoned cathedral now a fortress of power.

Rebuilt overnight.

Walls reinforced.

Stained glass glowing like a holy war.

Inside, rows of long black limousines carried kings and killers.

Politicians. Cartel bosses. Tech moguls. Elders from African dynasties. Everyone came to witness the funeral of a traitor whose bloodline bore the GrindTime name.

At the altar, a gold and obsidian casket gleamed beneath a massive stained-glass mural Eli, robed in fire and vines, surrounded by both serpents and saints.

Mama GrindTime arrived first, walking slowly, regal in a diamond-studded veil.

Then came King and his wife.

Dressed in all white. No weapon visible. Yet the most dangerous soul in the building.

Vinnie and Big Ty flanked him in black priest robes, each armed with concealed heavy artillery.

Ava moved quietly through the pews, relaying code through jeweled bracelets.

Gabi commanded the outer perimeter.

Jules linked the cathedral to GrindTime satellites above.

Dom sat mid-row, fingers tapping encrypted codes into his phone.

And in the front row?

Serenity.

She sat tall, with quiet fire in her eyes. Her black notebook clutched in her hands. On the front: “Royal Blood Never Fades.” Inside?

Her first poem.

A tribute.

A truth.

The Eulogy of a Betrayer

King stepped to the podium.

No microphone.

Just power.

"Loyalty ain't never about being perfect," he began, voice deep and clean. "It's about standing firm when the world tries to fold you. Eli forgot that."

Silence.

"But even betrayal... can water the roots of legacy."

Eyes scanned the room. He saw assassins. Presidents. Undercover D.E.A agents posing as clergy.

"Today, we buried a brother. Tomorrow, we baptize the world in justice."

He raised one finger to the heavens.

"One kingdom. One code. Long live the loyalty that never breaks even when blood does."

He stepped down.

Serenity stood up, calm like thunderclouds.

"My uncle lied... but I still loved him," she said softly. "This family? We grow through fire. We rise in the cracks. And no matter what comes at us..."

She looked up.

"We never fade."

The room didn't applaud. It wept.

Mama GrindTime kissed Serenity's forehead. "You just made the ancestors smile."

Thunder Cracks

Then came the sound.

Low... then louder.

A convoy of unmarked trucks screeched around the corner.

Gunfire.

Precise. Military. Planned.

An ambush during the funeral.

Vinnie flipped Serenity behind the hearse, already firing back with chrome-plated Uzis. Big Ty roared, pulled a grenade launcher from the casket's false bottom, and blew open the front gates.

King?

He didn't duck.

He stepped straight into the smoke with twin blades in hand, slicing through three mercenaries like they weren't even real.

Jules activated counter-drone systems.

Ava's bracelet blinked red, calling in allies from overseas.

Dom's war room tapped into local surveillance and jammed city signals. The cathedral turned into a war zone.

Then Serenity whispered, “Now.”

The church doors exploded outward.

Flames. Gas. Lockdown vents.

The attackers came fast and brutally tactical, global, and silent.

But they didn’t expect the cathedral to be a fortress.

In seven minutes, they were erased.

No names spoken. No flags waved.

Just a flash drive left in the rubble... and on it stated.

CLASSIFIED INTEL CODE NAME: KILL SWITCH

- Operative Status: ACTIVE
- Origin: Unknown
- Infiltration Level: GLOBAL
- Known Affiliates: [REDACTED]
- Primary Target: GrindTime Familia
- Outcome: FAILURE

One thing was certain the Familia’s knew this wasn’t over.

Big Ty looked over at King and Vinnie

“We need to know what groups were bold enough to step to the throne and still get laid down like they mama should have done.”

King wiped his blade nodding in agreement with Big Ty while Vinnie loaded more rounds into his dual pistols saying,

“They don’t know the war within they just created.”

As the GrindTime Familia stood over the last body they spoke out together saying all taking turns shooting his corpse.

“Royal Blood Never Fades.”

Not a single GrindTime soldier fell.

The street reeked of gunpowder and blood.

As dusk fell, Eli’s casket was lowered into the ground beneath the cathedral surrounded by roses, gun shells, and silence.

Mama GrindTime dropped a black rose.

Serenity dropped her notebook.

King stood at the edge of the grave.

No tears.

No words.

Just presence.

Just power.

He stared out at the city.

This is our city.

Columbus bowed in silence.

From Capitol Hill to cartel jungles, from betrayal to coronation, the message had been made clear:

You don't come for GrindTime and live.

The pyre rose behind them.

Eli's body burned.

Mama GrindTime lit it herself. "Let traitors see their end," she said.

Then she turned to King.

Kissed his forehead.

"You did what had to be done."

King turned to his family.

Serenity. Dom. Gabi. Ava.

Jules. Big Ty. Vinnie.

The bloodline.

The empire.

"The Foundation has been built and the world ain't seen nothin' yet, we will be global, let us always remember Royal Blood Never Fades" King said.

And behind King?

Fireworks erupted.

The war for the world had officially begun.

Authors Notes

Coming Soon - Volume Two

Royal Blood Never Fades: The War Within

The streets were only the beginning.

After betrayal within the family, an attempted assassination during Eli's funeral, and a war that spilled onto sacred ground. King GrindTime is done playing defense.

Volume Two kicks off with vengeance, expansion, and revelation.

From Columbus to Puerto Rico, Cuba to D.C., the GrindTime Empire sets its sights on global dominance from military, spiritual, economic, and generational.

The Church of the Unfaded rises.
New cartels emerge.
And the enemies?
They're no longer just in the streets...

They're in boardrooms, black sites, and bloodlines.

Dom builds the digital kingdom.
Jules taps into weapons hidden on the internet.
Serenity steps deeper into her inheritance.
And Mama GrindTime whispers the prophecy no one is ready for...

"Royal Blood doesn't just survive. It conquers."

About The Author

Daquian "GrindTime DQ" Williams is more than an author, he's a movement.

Born in Yonkers, New York, and raised in Columbus, Ohio, Daquian transformed pain into purpose, struggle into strategy, and dreams into dynasties. With a mind sharpened by hustle and a heart grounded in legacy, he's built an empire that spans publishing, staffing, music, entertainment, youth sports mentorship, community and mental health advocacy.

From battling the odds to breaking generational curses, his journey mirrors the same raw intensity and calculated power that fuels the Royal Blood Never Fades saga.

A father.

A leader.

A visionary.

GrindTime DQ has authored over ten books, including motivational journals, children's learning series, and gripping urban fiction. His stories are more than entertainment they're emotional awakenings designed to heal communities, spark ambition, and make people feel again.

Daquian holds three college degrees, owns seven plus corporations, and serves as a respected community leader, businessman and athletic coach, pouring wisdom into the next generation both on and off the field.

He is the founder of just to name a few:

- GrindTime Publishing Group Inc.
- Second Chance Elite Football Inc.
- BetterDays Nonprofit
- Grind Staffing Solutions
- Temple Of Serenity and Nature Laws
- and many more

Every venture he touches reflects a singular mission:

Build empires. Elevate minds. Break cycles.

And remind the world the moment you were born you were royal and that royal blood will never fade.

Follow his journey

Instagram:

@GrindTime_DQ

@GrindTimePublishingGroup

YouTube: GrindTime Entertainment

Email: grindtimepublishinggroup@gmail.com